THE JUNGLE OMNIBUS

Ruskin Bond has been writing for over sixty years, and has now over 120 titles in print—novels, collections of stories, poetry, essays, anthologies and books for children. His first novel, *The Room on the Roof*, received the prestigious John Llewellyn Rhys award in 1957. He has also received the Padma Shri (1999), the Padma Bhushan (2014) and two awards from the Sahitya Akademi—one for his short stories and another for his writings for children. In 2012, the Delhi government gave him its Lifetime Achievement Award.

Born in 1934, Ruskin Bond grew up in Jamnagar, Shimla, New Delhi and Dehradun. Apart from three years in the UK, he has spent all his life in India, and now lives in Mussoorie with his adopted family.

A shy person, Ruskin says he likes being a writer because 'When I'm writing there's nobody watching me. Today, it's hard to find a profession where you're not being watched!'

THE JUNGLE
OMNIBUS

RUSKIN BOND

RUPA

First published by
Rupa Publications India Pvt. Ltd 2014
7/16, Ansari Road, Daryaganj
New Delhi 110002

Sales Centres:

Allahabad Bengaluru Chennai
Hyderabad Jaipur Kathmandu
Kolkata Mumbai

ISBN: 978-81-291-2490-6

Second impression 2015

10 9 8 7 6 5 4 3 2

The moral right of the author has been asserted.

Printed at Gopsons Papers Ltd, Noida

For Dilip Guha, always giving my books to friends of all ages; long may he continue to be a familiar presence at Mussoorie's friendly neighbourhood bookshop.

CONTENTS

INTRODUCTION

~

The other day a young reader asked me: 'Sir, why do you write so many stores about leopards?'

I had to admit that leopards (or panthers, which are the same thing) often turn up in my stories, and for the simple reason that they keep turning up in my life. Tigers, on the other hand, are inclined to keep their distance, which is just as well, as I am no Jim Corbett.

Even as a boy, when every adult who possessed a gun seemed determined to boast of having shot a tiger or a leopard, or even a harmless elephant, the hunting of animals was distasteful to me. Live and let live was always my creed. My favourite shikari was the inebriated governor whose gun went off accidentally, the small shot penetrating a viceregal bottom, thus resulting in the postponement of a frontier war.

Tigers are shy, but not so leopards, who frequently prowl around hill stations, preying on pet dogs, goats, monkeys, and even poultry.

Up here in Landour, my friend and neighbour Rajvir Handa had a leopard over for dinner—the said dinner being his sturdy Bhutia Mastiff. Rajvir and the dog saw the leopard off. Mr Solomon wasn't so lucky. Out for an early morning walk with his Cocker Spaniel, he had not time to react when a hungry leopard sprang out from the bushes and carried off the dog, along with its collar and lead. This leopard preferred breakfast to dinner.

Over the years I have lost two dogs to leopards, so now I keep a cat. They say the cat is the aunt of the tiger and taught it everything—except how to climb a tree.

Tigers are heavy animals, more at home on the ground. But leopards are lithe, sinewy creatures, who have no difficulty climbing trees, rocky ledges, even rooftops. Late at night, I have often heard a leopard prowling on my old tin roof, probably in search of a sleeping monkey.

Very rarely do leopards or tigers attack humans. But with our towns and cities growing so rapidly, and eating into forest lands, there is bound to be some conflict between humans and the creatures of the wild. We must allow them their own space. They kill only for food. Humans kill for a large number of reasons—land, money, power, racial superiority, religion, all kinds of greed, passion and desire.

Animals have simple needs, and all they want is to be left alone. We are the interlopers.

Ruskin Bond
26 January 2014

NO ROOM FOR A LEOPARD

~

I first saw the leopard when I was crossing the small stream at the bottom of the hill. The ravine was so deep that for most of the day it remained in shadow. This encouraged many birds and animals to emerge from cover during the hours of daylight. Few people ever passed that way; only milkmen and charcoal burners from the surrounding villages. As a result, the ravine had become a little haven for wildlife, one of the few natural sanctuaries left near Mussoorie.

Below my cottage was a forest of oak and maple and Himalayan rhododendron. A narrow path twisted its way down through the trees, over an open ridge where red sorrel grew wild, and then down steeply through a tangle of wild raspberries, creeping vines and slender rangal bamboo. At the bottom of the hill a path led onto a grassy verge surrounded by wild dogroses. The streams ran close by the verge, tumbling over smooth pebbles, over rock worn yellow with age, on its way to the plains and to the little Song River and finally to the sacred Ganga.

Nearly every morning, and sometimes during the day, I heard the cry of the barking deer. And in the evening, walking through the forest, I disturbed parties of kalij pheasants. The birds went gliding into the ravines on open, motionless wings. I saw pine martins and a handsome red fox. I recognized the footprints of a bear.

As I had not come to take anything from the jungle, the birds and animals soon grew accustomed to my face. Or possibly they recognized my footsteps. After some time, my approach did not disturb them. A spotted forktail, which at first used to fly away, now remained perched on a boulder in the middle of the stream while I got across by means of other boulders only a few yards away.

The langurs in the oak and rhododendron trees who would at first go leaping through the branches at my approach, now watched me with some curiosity as they munched on the tender green shoots of the oak. The young ones scuffled and wrestled like boys while their parents groomed each other's coats, stretching themselves out on the sunlit hillside— beautiful animals with slim waists and long sinewy legs and tails full of character. But one evening, as I passed, I heard them chattering in the trees and I was not the cause of their excitement.

As I crossed the stream and began climbing the hill, the grunting and chattering increased, as though the langurs were trying to warn me of some hidden danger. A shower of pebbles came rattling down the steep hillside and I looked up to see a sinewy orange-gold leopard, poised on a rock about twenty feet above me.

It was not looking towards me but had its head thrust attentively forward in the direction of the ravine. It must have sensed my presence because it slowly turned its head and looked down at me. It seemed a little puzzled at my presence there, and when, to give myself courage, I clapped my hands sharply, the leopard sprang away into the thickets, making absolutely no sound as it melted into the shadows. I had disturbed the animal in its quest for food. But a little later, I heard the quickening cry of a barking deer as it fled through the forest—the hunt was still on.

The leopard, like other members of the cat family, is nearing extinction in India and I was surprised to find one so close to Mussoorie. Probably the deforestation that had been taking place in the surrounding hills had driven the deer into this green valley and the leopard, naturally, had followed.

It was some weeks before I saw the leopard again although I was often made aware of its presence. A dry rasping cough sometimes gave it away. At times I felt certain that I was being followed. And once, when I was late getting home, I was startled by a family of porcupines running about in a clearing. I looked around nervously and saw two bright eyes staring at me from a thicket. I stood still, my heart banging away against my ribs. Then the eyes danced away and I realized they were only fireflies.

In May and June, when the hills were brown and dry, it was always cool and green near the stream where ferns, maidenhair and long grasses continued to thrive.

One day I found the remains of a barking deer that had been partially eaten. I wondered why the leopard had not hidden the remains of his meal and decided that he had been disturbed while eating. Then climbing the hill, I met a party of shikaris resting beneath the oaks. They asked me if I had seen a leopard. I said I had not. They said they knew there was a leopard in the forest. Leopard skins, they told me, were selling in Delhi at over a thousand rupees each! Of course there was a ban on the export of its skins but they gave me to understand that there were ways and means... I thanked them for their information and moved on, feeling uneasy and disturbed.

The shikaris had seen the carcass of the deer and the leopard's pug marks and they kept coming to the forest. Almost every evening I heard their guns banging away, for they were ready to fire at almost everything.

'There's a leopard about,' they told me. 'You should carry a gun.'

'I don't have one,' I said.

There were fewer birds to be seen and even the langurs had moved on. The red fox did not show itself and the pine martins who had earlier become bold, now dashed into hiding at my approach. The smell of one human is like the smell of any other.

I thought no more of the men. My attitude towards them was similar to the attitude of the denizens of the forest—they were men, unpredictable and to be avoided if possible.

One day after crossing the stream, I climbed Pari Tibba, a bleak, scrub-covered hill where no one lived. This was a stiff undertaking, because there was no path to the top and I had to scramble up a precipitous rock-face with the help of rocks and roots which were apt to come away in my groping hand. But at the top was a plateau with a few pine trees, their upper branches catching the wind and humming softly. There I found the ruins of what must have been the first settlers— just a few piles of rubble now overgrown with weeds, sorrel, dandelion and nettles.

As I walked through the roofless ruins, I was struck by the silence that surrounded me, the absence of birds and animals, the sense of complete desolation. The silence was so absolute that it seemed to be shouting in my ears. But there was something else of which I was becoming increasingly aware—the strong feline odour of one of the cat family. I paused and looked about. I was alone. There was no movement of dry leaf or loose stone. The ruins were, for the most part, open to the sky. Their rotting rafters had collapsed and joined together to form a low passage, like the entrance to a mine. This dark cavern seemed to lead down.

The smell was stronger when I approached this spot so I stopped again and waited there, wondering if I had discovered the lair of the leopard, wondering if the animal was now at rest after a night's hunt. Perhaps it was crouched there in the dark, watching me, recognizing me, knowing me as a man who walked alone in the forest without a weapon. I like to think that he was there and that he knew me and that he acknowledged my visit in the friendliest way—by ignoring me altogether.

Perhaps I had made him confident—too confident, too

careless, too trusting of the human in his midst. I did not venture any further. I did not seek physical contact or even another glimpse of that beautiful sinewy body, springing from rock to rock... It was his trust I wanted and I think he gave it to me. But did the leopard, trusting one man, make the mistake of bestowing his trust on others? Did I, by casting out all fear—my own fear and the leopard's protective fear— leave him defenceless?

Because next day, coming up the path from the stream, shouting and beating their drums, were the shikaris. They had a long bamboo pole across their shoulder and slung from the pole, feet up, head down, was the lifeless body of the leopard. It had been shot in the neck and in the head.

'We told you there was a leopard!' they shouted, in great good humour. 'Isn't he a fine specimen?'

'Yes,' I said. 'He was a beautiful leopard.'

I walked home through the silent forest. It was very silent, almost as though the birds and animals knew their trust had been violated.

I remembered the lines of a poem by D.H. Lawrence and as I climbed the steep and lonely path to my home, the words beat out their rhythm in my mind—'There was room in the world for a mountain lion and me.'

ROMI AND THE WILDFIRE

~

1

As Romi was about to mount his bicycle, he saw smoke rising from behind the distant line of trees.

'It looks like a forest fire,' said Prem, his friend and classmate.

'It's well to the east,' said Romi. 'Nowhere near the road.'

'There's a strong wind,' said Prem, looking at the dry leaves swirling across the road.

It was the middle of May, and it hadn't rained in the Terai for several weeks. The grass was brown, the leaves of the trees covered with dust. Even though it was getting on to six o'clock in the evening, the boys' shirts were damp with sweat.

'It will be getting dark soon,' said Prem. 'You'd better spend the night at my house.'

'No, I said I'd be home tonight. My father isn't keeping

well. The doctor has given me some tablets for him.'

'You'd better hurry, then. That fire seems to be spreading.'

'Oh, it's far off. It will take me only forty minutes to ride through the forest. Bye, Prem. See you tomorrow!'

Romi mounted his bicycle and pedalled off down the main road of the village, scattering stray hens, stray dogs and stray villagers.

'Hey, look where you're going!' shouted an angry villager, leaping out of the way of the oncoming bicycle. 'Do you think you own the road?'

'Of course I own it,' called Romi cheerfully, and cycled on.

His own village lay about seven miles distant, on the other side of the forest; but there was only a primary school in his village, and Romi was now in high school. His father, who was a fairly wealthy sugarcane farmer, had only recently bought him the bicycle. Romi didn't care too much for school and felt there weren't enough holidays; but he enjoyed the long rides, and he got on well with his classmates.

He might have stayed the night with Prem had it not been for the tablets which the vaid—the village doctor—had given him for his father.

Romi's father was having back trouble, and the medicine had been specially prepared from local herbs.

Having been given such a fine bicycle, Romi felt that the least he could do in return was to get those tablets to his father as early as possible.

He put his head down and rode swiftly out of the village. Ahead of him, the smoke rose from the burning forest and the sky glowed red.

2

He had soon left the village far behind. There was a slight climb, and Romi had to push harder on the pedals to get over the rise. Once over the top, the road went winding down to the edge of the subtropical forest.

This was the part Romi enjoyed most. He relaxed, stopped pedalling, and allowed the bicycle to glide gently down the slope. Soon the wind was rushing past him, blowing his hair about his face and making his shirt billow out behind. He burst into song.

A dog from the village ran beside him, barking furiously. Romi shouted to the dog, encouraging him in the race.

Then the road straightened out, and Romi began pedalling again.

The dog, seeing the forest ahead, turned back to the village. It was afraid of the forest.

The smoke was thicker now, and Romi caught the smell of burning timber. But ahead of him the road was clear. He rode on.

It was a rough, dusty road, cut straight through the forest. Tall trees grew on either side, cutting off the last of the daylight. But the spreading glow of the fire on the right lit up the road, and giant tree-shadows danced before the boy on the bicycle.

Usually the road was deserted. This evening it was alive with wild creatures fleeing from the forest fire.

The first animal that Romi saw was a hare, leaping across the road in front of him. It was followed by several more hares.

Then a band of monkeys streamed across, chattering excitedly.

They'll be safe on the other side, thought Romi. The fire won't cross the road.

But it was coming closer. And realizing this, Romi pedalled harder. In half-an-hour he should be out of the forest.

Suddenly, from the side of the road, several pheasants rose in the air, and with a *whoosh*, flew low across the path, just in front of the oncoming bicycle. Taken by surprise, Romi fell off. When he picked himself up and began brushing his clothes, he saw that his knee was bleeding. It wasn't a deep cut, but he allowed it to bleed a little, took out his handkerchief and bandaged his knee. Then he mounted the bicycle again.

He rode a bit slower now, because birds and animals kept coming out of the bushes.

Not only pheasants but smaller birds, too, were streaming across the road—parrots, jungle crows, owls, magpies—and the air was filled with their cries.

'Everyone's on the move,' thought Romi. It must be a really big fire.

He could see the flames now, reaching out from behind the trees on his right, and he could hear the crackling as the dry leaves caught fire. The air was hot on his face. Leaves, still alight or turning to cinders, floated past.

A herd of deer crossed the road, and Romi had to stop until they had passed. Then he mounted again and rode on; but now, for the first time, he was feeling afraid.

3

From ahead came a faint clanging sound. It wasn't an animal sound, Romi was sure of that. A fire engine? There were no fire engines within fifty miles.

The clanging came nearer, and Romi discovered that the noise came from a small boy who was running along the forest path, two milk cans clattering at his side

'Teju!' called Romi, recognizing the boy from a neighbouring village. 'What are you doing out here?'

'Trying to get home, of course,' said Teju, panting along beside the bicycle.

'Jump on,' said Romi, stopping for him.

Teju was only eight or nine—a couple of years younger than Romi. He had come to deliver milk to some road workers, but the workers had left at the first signs of the fire, and Teju was hurrying home with his cans still full of milk.

He got up on the crossbar of the bicycle, and Romi moved on again. He was quite used to carrying friends on the crossbar.

'Keep beating your milk cans,' said Romi. 'Like that, the animals will know we are coming. My bell doesn't make enough noise. I'm going to get a horn for my cycle!'

'I never knew there were so many animals in the jungle,' said Teju. 'I saw a python in the middle of the road. It stretched right across!'

'What did you do?'

'Just kept running and jumped right over it!'

Teju continued to chatter but Romi's thoughts were on the fire, which was much closer now. Flames shot up from the dry grass and ran up the trunks of trees and along the branches. Smoke billowed out above the forest.

Romi's eyes were smarting and his hair and eyebrows felt scorched. He was feeling tired but he couldn't stop now, he had to get beyond the range of the fire. Another ten or fifteen minutes of steady riding would get them to the small wooden bridge that spanned the little river separating the forest from the sugarcane fields.

Once across the river, they would be safe. The fire could not touch them on the other side, because the forest ended at the river's edge. But could they get to the river in time?

4

Clang, clang, clang, went Teju's milk cans. But the sound of the fire grew louder too.

A tall silk-cotton tree, its branches leaning across the road, had caught fire. They were almost beneath it when there was a crash and a burning branch fell to the ground a few yards in front of them.

The boys had to get off the bicycle and leave the road, forcing their way through a tangle of thorny bushes on the left, dragging and pushing at the bicycle and only returning to the road some distance ahead of the burning tree.

'We won't get out in time,' said Teju, back on the crossbar but feeling disheartened.

'Yes, we will,' said Romi, pedalling with all his might. 'The fire hasn't crossed the road as yet.'

Even as he spoke, he saw a small flame leap up from

the grass on the left. It wouldn't be long before more sparks and burning leaves were blown across the road to kindle the grass on the other side.

'Oh, look!' exclaimed Romi, bringing the bicycle to a sudden stop.

'What's wrong now?' asked Teju, rubbing his sore eyes. And then, through the smoke, he saw what was stopping them.

An elephant was standing in the middle of the road.

Teju slipped off the crossbar, his cans rolling on the ground, bursting open and spilling their contents.

The elephant was about forty feet away. It moved about restlessly, its big ears flapping as it turned its head from side to side, wondering which way to go.

From far to the left, where the forest was still untouched, a herd of elephants moved towards the river. The leader of the herd raised his trunk and trumpeted a call. Hearing it, the elephant in the road raised its own trunk and trumpeted a reply. Then it shambled off into the forest, in the direction of the herd, leaving the way clear.

'Come, Teju, jump on!' urged Romi. 'We can't stay here much longer!'

Teju forgot about his milk cans and pulled himself up on the crossbar. Romi ran forward with the bicycle, to gain speed, and mounted swiftly. He kept as far as possible to the left of the road, trying to ignore the flames, the crackling, the smoke and the scorching heat.

It seemed that all the animals who could get away had done so. The exodus across the road had stopped.

'We won't stop again,' said Romi, gritting his teeth. 'Not

even for an elephant!'

'We're nearly there!' said Teju. He was perking up again.

A jackal, overcome by the heat and smoke, lay in the middle of the path, either dead or unconscious. Romi did not stop. He swerved round the animal. Then he put all his strength into one final effort.

He covered the last hundred yards at top speed, and then they were out of the forest, free-wheeling down the sloping road to the river.

'Look!' shouted Teju. 'The bridge is on fire!'

Burning embers had floated down on to the small wooden bridge, and the dry, ancient timber had quickly caught fire. It was now burning fiercely.

Romi did not hesitate. He left the road, riding the bicycle over sand and pebbles. Then, with a rush, they went down the river bank and into the water.

The next thing they knew they were splashing around, trying to find each other in the darkness. 'Help!' cried Teju. 'I'm drowning!'

5

'Don't be silly,' said Romi. 'The water isn't deep—it's only up to the knees. Come here and grab hold of me.'

Teju splashed across and grabbed Romi by the belt.

'The water's so cold,' he said, his teeth chattering.

'Do you want to go back and warm yourself?' asked Romi. 'Some people are never satisfied. Come on, help me get the bicycle up. It's down here, just where we are standing.'

Together they managed to heave the bicycle out of the water and stand it upright.

'Now sit on it,' said Romi. 'I'll push you across.'

'We'll be swept away,' said Teju.

'No, we won't. There's not much water in the river at this time of the year. But the current is quite strong in the middle, so sit still. All right?'

'All right,' said Teju nervously.

Romi began guiding the bicycle across the river, one hand on the seat and one hand on the handlebar. The river was shallow and sluggish in midsummer; even so, it was quite swift in the middle. But having got safely out of the burning forest, Romi was in no mood to let a little river defeat him.

He kicked off his shoes, knowing they would be lost; and then gripping the smooth stones of the river-bed with his toes, he concentrated on keeping his balance and getting the bicycle and Teju through the middle of the stream. The water here came up to his waist, and the current would have been too strong for Teju. But when they reached the shallows, Teju got down and helped Romi push the bicycle.

They reached the opposite bank, and sank down on the grass.

'We can rest now,' said Romi. 'But not all night—I've got some medicine to give to my father.' He felt in his pockets and found that the tablets in their envelope, had turned into a soggy mess. 'Oh well, he had to take them with water anyway,' he said.

They watched the fire as it continued to spread through the forest. It had crossed the road down which they had come. The sky was a bright red, and the river reflected the colour of the sky.

Several elephants had found their way down to the river. They were cooling off by spraying water on each other with their trunks. Further downstream, there were deer and other animals.

Romi and Teju looked at each other in the glow from the fire. They hadn't known each other very well before. But now they felt they had been friends for years.

'What are you thinking about?' asked Teju.

'I'm thinking,' said Romi, 'that even if the fire is out in a day or two, it will be a long time before the bridge is repaired. So it will be a nice long holiday from school!'

'But you can walk across the river,' said Teju. 'You just did it.'

'Impossible,' said Romi. 'It's much too swift.'

BUTTERFLY TIME

~

April showers
Bring swarms of butterflies
Streaming across the valley
Seeking sweet nectar.
Yellow, gold, and burning bright,
Red and blue and banded white.
To my eyes they bring delight!
Theirs a long and arduous flight,
Here today and off tomorrow,
Floating on, bright butterflies,
To distant bowers.
For Nature does things in good order:
And birds and butterflies recognize
No man-made border.

UNCLE KEN'S RUMBLE
IN THE JUNGLE

~

Uncle Ken drove Grandfather's old Fiat along the forest road at an incredible 30 mph. scattering pheasants, partridges and jungle fowl as he scattered along. He had come in search of the disappearing Red Jungle Fowl, and I could see why the bird had disappeared. Too many noisy human beings had invaded its habitat.

By the time we reached the forest rest house, one of the car doors had fallen off its hinges, and a large lantana bush had got entwined in the bumper.

'Never mind,' said Uncle Ken. 'It's all part of the adventure.'

The rest house had been reserved for Uncle Ken, thanks to Grandfather's good relations with the forest department. But I was the only other person in the car. No one else would trust himself or herself to Uncle Ken's driving. He treated a car as though it were a low-flying aircraft having some difficulty in getting of the runway.

As we arrived at the rest house, a number of hens made a dash for safety.

'Look, jungle fowl!' exclaimed Uncle Ken.

'Domestic fowl,' I said. 'They must belong to the forest guards.'

I was right, of course. One of the hens was destined to be served up as chicken curry later that day. The jungle birds avoided the neighbourhood of the rest house, just in case they were mistaken for poultry and went into the cooking pot.

Uncle Ken was all for starting his search right away, and after a brief interval during which we were served tea and pakoras (prepared by the forest guard, who it turned out was also a good cook), we set off on foot into the jungle in search of the elusive Red Jungle Fowl.

'No tigers around here, are there?' asked Uncle Ken, just to be on the safe side.

'No tigers on this range,' said the guard. 'Just elephants.'

Uncle Ken wasn't afraid of elephants. He'd been on numerous elephants rides at the Lucknow zoo. He'd also seen Sabu in *Elephant Boy*.

A small wooden bridge took us across a little river, and then we were in the jungle, following the forest guard who led us along a path that was frequently blocked by broken tree branches and pieces of bamboo.

'Why all these broken branches?' asked Uncle Ken.

'The elephants, sir,' replied our guard. 'They passed through last night. They like certain leaves, as well as young bamboo shoots.'

We saw a number of spotted deer and several pheasants, but no Red Jungle Fowl.

That evening, we sat out on the veranda of the rest house. All was silent except for the distant trumpeting of elephants. Then, from the stream, came the chanting of hundreds of frogs.

There were tenors and baritones, sopranos and contraltos, and occasionally a bass deep enough to have pleased the great Chaliapin. They sang duets and quartets from *La Bohème* and other Italian operas, drowsing out all other jungle sounds except for the occasional cry of a jackal doing his best to join in.

'We might as well sing too,' said Uncle Ken, and began singing 'Indian Love Call' in his best Nelson Eddy manner.

The frogs fell silent, obviously awestruck; but instead of receiving an answering love call, Uncle Ken was answered by even more strident jackal calls—not one, but several—with the result that all self-respecting denizens of the forest fled from the vicinity, and we saw no wildlife that night apart from a frightened rabbit that sped across the clearing and vanished into the darkness.

Early next morning, we renewed our efforts to track down the Red Jungle Fowl, but it remained elusive. Returning to the rest house dusty and weary, Uncle Ken exclaimed: 'There it is—a Red Jungle Fowl.'

But it turned out to be the caretaker's cock bird, a handsome fellow all red and gold, but not the jungle variety.

Disappointed, Uncle Ken decided to return to civilization. Another night in the rest house did not appeal to him. He had run out of songs to sing.

In any case, the weather had changed overnight and a

light drizzle was falling as we started out. This had turned to a steady downpour by the time we reached the bridge across the Suseva river. And standing in the middle of the bridge was an elephant.

He was a long tusker and he didn't look too friendly.

Uncle Ken blew his horn, and that was a mistake.

It was a strident, penetrating horn, highly effective on city roads but out of place in the forest.

The elephant took it as a challenge, and returned the blast of the horn with a shrill trumpeting of its own. It took a few steps forward. Uncle Ken put the car into reverse.

'Is there another way out of here?' he asked.

'There's a side road,' I said, recalling an earlier trip with Grandfather. 'It will take us to the Kansrao railway station.'

'What, ho!' cried Uncle Ken. 'To the station we go!'

And he turned the car and drove back until we came to the turning.

The narrow road was now a rushing torrent of rain water and all Uncle Ken's driving skills were put to the test. He had on one occasion driven through a brick wall, so he knew all about obstacles; but they were usually stationary ones.

'More elephants,' I said, as two large pachyderms loomed out of the rain-drenched forest.

'Elephants to the right of us, elephants to the left of us!' chanted Uncle Ken, misquoting Tennyson's 'Charge of the Light Brigade'. 'Into the valley of death rode the six hundred!'

'There are now three of them,' I observed.

'Not my lucky number,' said Uncle Ken and pressed hard on the accelerator. We lurched forward, almost running over a terrified barking deer.

'Is four your lucky number, Uncle Ken?'

'Why do you ask?'

'Well, there are now four of them behind us. And they are catching up quite fast!'

'I see the station ahead,' cried Uncle Ken, as we drove into a clearing where a tiny railway station stood like a beacon of safety in the wilderness.

The car came to a grinding halt. We abandoned it and ran for the building.

The stationmaster saw our predicament, and beckoned to us to enter the station building, which was little more than a two-room shed and platform. He took us inside his tiny control room and shut the steel gate behind us.

'The elephants won't bother you here,' he said. 'But say goodbye to your car.'

We looked out of the window and were horrified to see Grandfather's Fiat overturned by one of the elephants, while another proceeded to trample it underfoot. The other elephants joined in the mayhem and soon the car was a flattened piece of junk.

'I'm stationmaster Abdul Ranf,' the stationmaster introduced himself. 'I know a good scrap dealer in Doiwala. I'll give you his address.'

'But how do we get out of here?' asked Uncle Ken.

'Well, it's only an hour's walk to Doiwala, but not with those elephants around. Stay and have a cup of tea. The Dehra Express will pass through shortly. It stops for a few minutes. And it's only half-an-hour to Dehra from here.' He punched out a couple of rail tickets. 'Here you are, my friends. Just two rupees each. The cheapest rail journey in India. And these tickets carry an insurance value of two lakh rupees each, should an accident befall you between here and Dehradun.'

Uncle Ken's eyes lit up.

'You mean, if one of us falls out of the train?' he asked.

'Out of the moving train,' clarified the stationmaster. 'There will be an enquiry, of course, some people try to fake an accident.'

But Uncle Ken decided against falling out of the train and making a fortune. He'd had enough excitement for the day. We got home safely enough, taking a pony cart from Dehradun station to our house.

'Where's my car?' asked Grandfather, as we staggered up the veranda steps.

'It had a small accident,' said Uncle Ken. 'We left it outside the Kansrao railway station. I'll collect it later.'

'I'm starving,' I said. 'Haven't eaten since morning.'

'Well, come and have your dinner,' said Granny. 'I've made something special for you. One of your grandfather's hunting friends sent us a jungle fowl. I've made a nice roast. Try it with apple sauce.'

Uncle Ken did not ask if the jungle fowl was red, grey, or technicoloured. He was the first to the dining table.

Granny had anticipated this, and served me with a chicken leg, giving the other leg to Grandfather.

'I rather fancy the breast myself,' she said, and this left Uncle Ken with a long and scrawny neck—which was more than he deserved.

PANTHER'S MOON

~

1

In the entire village, he was the first to get up. Even the dog, a big hill mastiff called Sheroo, was asleep in a corner of the dark room, curled up near the cold embers of the previous night's fire. Bisnu's tousled head emerged from his blanket. He rubbed the sleep from his eyes and sat up on his haunches. Then, gathering his wits, he crawled in the direction of the loud ticking that came from the battered little clock which occupied the second-most honoured place in a niche in the wall. The most honoured place belonged to a picture of Ganesha, the god of learning, who had an elephant's head and a fat boy's body.

Bringing his face close to the clock, Bisnu could just make out the hands. It was five o'clock. He had half an hour in which to get ready and leave.

He got up, in vest and underpants, and moved quietly towards the door. The soft tread of his bare feet woke Sheroo, and the big black dog rose silently and padded behind the boy. The door opened and closed, and then the boy and the dog were outside in the early dawn. The month was June, and the nights were warm, even in the Himalayan valleys, but there was fresh dew on the grass. Bisnu felt the dew beneath his feet. He took a deep breath and began walking down to the stream.

The sound of the stream filled the small valley. At that early hour of the morning, it was the only sound, but Bisnu was hardly conscious of it. It was a sound he lived with and took for granted. It was only when he had crossed the hill, on his way to the town—and the sound of the stream grew distant—that he really began to notice it. And it was only when the stream was too far away to be heard that he really missed its sound.

He slipped out of his underclothes, gazed for a few moments at the goose pimples rising on his flesh, and then dashed into the shallow stream. As he went further in, the cold mountain water reached his loins and navel, and he gasped with shock and pleasure. He drifted slowly with the current, swam across to a small inlet which formed a fairly deep pool, and plunged into the water. Sheroo hated cold water at this early hour. Had the sun been up, he would not have hesitated to join Bisnu. Now he contented himself with sitting on a smooth rock and gazing placidly at the slim brown boy splashing about in the clear water in the widening light of dawn.

Bisnu did not stay long in the water. There wasn't time. When he returned to the house, he found his mother up, making tea and chapattis. His sister, Puja, was still asleep. She was a little older than Bisnu, a pretty girl with large black eyes, good teeth and strong arms and legs. During the day, she helped her mother in the house and in the fields. She did not go to the school with Bisnu. But when he came home in the evenings, he would try teaching her some of the things he had learnt. Their father was dead. Bisnu, at twelve, considered himself the head of the family.

He ate two chapattis, after spreading butter-oil on them. He drank a glass of hot sweet tea. His mother gave two thick chapattis to Sheroo, and the dog wolfed them down in a few minutes. Then she wrapped two chapattis and some gourd curry in some big green leaves, and handed these to Bisnu. This was his lunch packet. His mother and Puja would take their meal afterwards.

When Bisnu was dressed, he stood with folded hands before the picture of Ganesha. Ganesha is the god who blesses all beginnings. The author who begins to write a new book, the banker who opens a new ledger, the traveller who starts on a journey, all invoke the kindly help of Ganesha. And as Bisnu made a journey every day, he never left without the goodwill of the elephant-headed god.

How, one might ask, did Ganesha get his elephant's head?

When born, he was a beautiful child. Parvati, his mother, was so proud of him that she went about showing him to everyone. Unfortunately she made the mistake of showing the child to that envious planet, Saturn, who promptly burnt off poor Ganesha's head. Parvati, in despair, went to Brahma, the Creator, for a new head for her son. He had no head to give her, but advised her to search for some man or animal caught in a sinful or wrong act. Parvati wandered about until she came upon an elephant sleeping with its head the wrong way, that is, to the south. She promptly removed the elephant's head and planted it on Ganesha's shoulders, where it took root.

Bisnu knew this story. He had heard it from his mother.

Wearing a white shirt and black shorts, and a pair of worn white keds, he was ready for his long walk to school, five miles up the mountain.

His sister woke up just as he was about to leave. She pushed the hair away from her face and gave Bisnu one of her rare smiles.

'I hope you have not forgotten,' she said.

'Forgotten?' said Bisnu, pretending innocence. 'Is there anything I am supposed to remember?'

'Don't tease me. You promised to buy me a pair of bangles, remember? I hope you won't spend the money on sweets, as you did last time.'

'Oh, yes, your bangles,' said Bisnu. 'Girls have nothing better to do than waste money on trinkets. Now, don't lose your temper! I'll get them for you. Red and gold are the colours you want?'

'Yes, Bhaiya,' said Puja gently, pleased that Bisnu had remembered the colours. 'And for your dinner tonight, we'll make you something special. Won't we, Mother?'

'Yes. But hurry up and get dressed. There is some ploughing

to be done today. The rains will soon be here, if the gods are kind.'

'The monsoon will be late this year,' said Bisnu. 'Mr Nautiyal, our teacher, told us so. He said it had nothing to do with the gods.'

'Be off, you are getting late,' said Puja, before Bisnu could begin an argument with his mother. She was diligently winding the old clock. It was quite light in the room. The sun would be up any minute.

Bisnu shouldered his school bag, kissed his mother, pinched his sister's cheeks and left the house. He started climbing the steep path up the mountainside. Sheroo bounded ahead; for he, too, always went with Bisnu to school.

Five miles to school. Every day, except Sunday, Bisnu walked five miles to school; and in the evening, he walked home again. There was no school in his own small village of Manjari, for the village consisted of only five families. The nearest school was at Kemptee, a small township on the bus route through the district of Garhwal. A number of boys walked to school, from distances of two or three miles; their villages were not quite as remote as Manjari. But Bisnu's village lay right at the bottom of the mountain, a drop of over two thousand feet from Kemptee. There was no proper road between the village and the town.

In Kemptee there was a school, a small mission hospital, a post office and several shops. In Manjari village there were none of these amenities. If you were sick, you stayed at home until you got well; if you were very sick, you walked or were carried to the hospital, up the five-mile path. If you wanted to buy something, you went without it; but if you wanted it very badly, you could walk the five miles to Kemptee.

Manjari was known as the Five-Mile Village.

Twice a week, if there were any letters, a postman came to the village. Bisnu usually passed the postman on his way to and from school.

There were other boys in Manjari village, but Bisnu was the only one who went to school. His mother would not have fussed if he had stayed at home and worked in the fields. That was what the other boys did; all except lazy Chittru, who preferred fishing in the stream or helping himself to the fruit off other people's trees. But Bisnu went to school. He went because he wanted to. No one could force him to go; and no one could stop him from going. He had set his heart on receiving a good schooling. He wanted to read and write as well as anyone in the big world, the world that seemed to begin only where the mountains ended. He felt cut off from the world in his small valley. He would rather live at the top of a mountain than at the bottom of one. That was why he liked climbing to Kemptee, it took him to the top of the mountain; and from its ridge he could look down on his own valley to the north, and on the wide endless plains stretching towards the south.

The plainsman looks to the hills for the needs of his spirit but the hill man looks to the plains for a living.

Leaving the village and the fields below him, Bisnu climbed steadily up the bare hillside, now dry and brown. By the time the sun was up, he had entered the welcome shade of an oak and rhododendron forest. Sheroo went bounding ahead, chasing squirrels and barking at langurs.

A colony of langurs lived in the oak forest. They fed on oak leaves, acorns and other green things, and usually remained in the trees, coming down to the ground only to play or bask in the sun. They were beautiful, supple-limbed animals, with black faces and silver-grey coats and long, sensitive tails. They leapt from tree to tree with great agility. The young ones wrestled on the grass like boys.

A dignified community, the langurs did not have the cheekiness or dishonest habits of the red monkeys of the plains; they did not approach dogs or humans. But they had grown used to Bisnu's comings and goings, and did not fear him. Some of the older ones would watch him quietly, a little puzzled. They did not go near the town, because the Kemptee boys threw stones at them. And anyway, the oak forest gave them all the food they required.

Emerging from the trees, Bisnu crossed a small brook. Here he stopped to drink the fresh clean water of a spring. The brook tumbled down the mountain and joined the river a little below Bisnu's village. Coming from another direction was a second path, and at the junction of the two paths Sarru was waiting for him.

Sarru came from a small village about three miles from Bisnu's and closer to the town. He had two large milk cans slung over his shoulders. Every morning he carried this milk to town, selling one can to the school and the other to Mrs Taylor, the lady doctor at the small mission hospital. He was a little older than Bisnu but not as well-built.

They hailed each other, and Sarru fell into step beside

Bisnu. They often met at this spot, keeping each other company for the remaining two miles to Kemptee.

'There was a panther in our village last night,' said Sarru.

This information interested but did not excite Bisnu. Panthers were common enough in the hills and did not usually present a problem except during the winter months, when their natural prey was scarce. Then, occasionally, a panther would take to haunting the outskirts of a village, seizing a careless dog or a stray goat.

'Did you lose any animals?' asked Bisnu.

'No. It tried to get into the cowshed but the dogs set up an alarm. We drove it off.'

'It must be the same one which came around last winter. We lost a calf and two dogs in our village.'

'Wasn't that the one the shikaris wounded? I hope it hasn't become a cattle lifter.'

'It could be the same. It has a bullet in its leg. These hunters are the people who cause all the trouble. They think it's easy to shoot a panther. It would be better if they missed altogether, but they usually wound it.'

'And then the panther's too slow to catch the barking deer, and starts on our own animals.'

'We're lucky it didn't become a man-eater. Do you remember the man-eater six years ago? I was very small then. My father told me all about it. Ten people were killed in our valley alone. What happened to it?'

'I don't know. Some say it poisoned itself when it ate the headman of another village.'

Bisnu laughed. 'No one liked that old villain. He must have

been a man-eater himself in some previous existence!' They linked arms and scrambled up the stony path. Sheroo began barking and ran ahead. Someone was coming down the path.

It was Mela Ram, the postman.

2

'Any letters for us?' asked Bisnu and Sarru together.

They never received any letters but that did not stop them from asking. It was one way of finding out who had received letters.

'You're welcome to all of them,' said Mela Ram. 'If you'll carry my bag for me.'

'Not today,' said Sarru. 'We're busy today. Is there a letter from Corporal Ghanshyam for his family?'

'Yes, there is a postcard for his people. He is posted on the Ladakh border now and finds it very cold there.'

Postcards, unlike sealed letters, were considered public property and were read by everyone. The senders knew that too, and so Corporal Ghanshyam Singh was careful to mention that he expected a promotion very soon. He wanted everyone in his village to know it.

Mela Ram, complaining of sore feet, continued on his way, and the boys carried on up the path. It was eight o'clock when they reached Kemptee. Dr Taylor's outpatients were just beginning to trickle in at the hospital gate. The doctor was trying to prop up a rose creeper which had blown down during the night. She liked attending to her plants in the mornings, before starting on her patients. She found this helped her in her work. There was a lot in common between ailing plants and ailing people.

Dr Taylor was fifty, white-haired but fresh in the face and full of vitality. She had been in India for twenty years, and ten of these had been spent working in the hill regions.

She saw Bisnu coming down the road. She knew about the boy and his long walk to school and admired him for his keenness and sense of purpose. She wished there were more like him.

Bisnu greeted her shyly. Sheroo barked and put his paws up on the gate.

'Yes, there's a bone for you,' said Dr Taylor. She often put aside bones for the big black dog, for she knew that Bisnu's people could not afford to give the dog a regular diet of meat—though he did well enough on milk and chapattis.

She threw the bone over the gate and Sheroo caught it before it fell. The school bell began ringing and Bisnu broke into a run. Sheroo loped along behind the boy.

When Bisnu entered the school gate, Sheroo sat down on the grass of the compound. He would remain there until the lunch break. He knew of various ways of amusing himself during school hours and had friends among the bazaar dogs. But just then he didn't want company. He had his bone to get on with.

Mr Nautiyal, Bisnu's teacher, was in a bad mood. He was a keen rose grower and only that morning, on getting up and looking out of his bedroom window, he had been horrified to see a herd of goats in his garden. He had chased them down the road with a stick but the damage had already been done.

His prize roses had all been consumed.

Mr Nautiyal had been so upset that he had gone without his breakfast. He had also cut himself whilst shaving. Thus, his mood had gone from bad to worse. Several times during the day, he brought down his ruler on the knuckles of any boy who irritated him. Bisnu was one of his best pupils. But even Bisnu irritated him by asking too many questions about a new sum which Mr Nautiyal didn't feel like explaining.

That was the kind of day it was for Mr Nautiyal. Most schoolteachers know similar days.

'Poor Mr Nautiyal,' thought Bisnu. 'I wonder why he's so upset. It must be because of his pay. He doesn't get much money. But he's a good teacher. I hope he doesn't take another job.' But after Mr Nautiyal had eaten his lunch, his mood improved (as it always did after a meal), and the rest of the day passed serenely. Armed with a bundle of homework, Bisnu came out from the school compound at four o'clock, and was immediately joined by Sheroo. He proceeded down the road in the company of several of his classfellows. But he did not linger long in the bazaar. There were five miles to walk, and he did not like to get home too late. Usually, he reached his house just as it was beginning to get dark. Sarru had gone home long ago, and Bisnu had to make the return journey on his own. It was a good opportunity to memorize the words of an English poem he had been asked to learn.

Bisnu had reached the little brook when he remembered the bangles he had promised to buy for his sister.

'Oh, I've forgotten them again,' he said aloud. 'Now I'll catch it—and she's probably made something special for my dinner!'

Sheroo, to whom these words were addressed, paid no attention but bounded off into the oak forest. Bisnu looked around for the monkeys but they were nowhere to be seen.

'Strange,' he thought. 'I wonder why they have disappeared.' He was startled by a sudden sharp cry, followed by a fierce yelp. He knew at once that Sheroo was in trouble. The noise came from the bushes down the khud into which the dog had rushed but a few seconds previously.

Bisnu jumped off the path and ran down the slope towards the bushes. There was no dog and not a sound. He whistled and called, but there was no response. Then he saw something lying on the dry grass. He picked it up. It was a portion of a dog's collar, stained with blood. It was Sheroo's collar and Sheroo's blood.

Bisnu did not search further. He knew, without a doubt, that Sheroo had been seized by a panther. No other animal could have attacked so silently and swiftly and carried off a big dog without a struggle. Sheroo was dead—must have been dead within seconds of being caught and flung into the air. Bisnu knew the danger that lay in wait for him if he followed the blood trail through the trees. The panther would attack anyone who interfered with its meal. With tears starting in his eyes, Bisnu carried on down the path to the village. His fingers still clutched the little bit of bloodstained collar that was all that was left of his dog.

3

Bisnu was not a very sentimental boy, but he sorrowed for

his dog, who had been his companion on many a hike into the hills and forests. He did not sleep that night, but turned restlessly from side to side moaning softly. After some time he felt Puja's hand on his head. She began stroking his brow. He took her hand in his own and the clasp of her rough, warm, familiar hand gave him a feeling of comfort and security.

Next morning, when he went down to the stream to bathe, he missed the presence of his dog. He did not stay long in the water. It wasn't as much fun when there was no Sheroo to watch him.

When Bisnu's mother gave him his food, she told him to be careful and hurry home that evening. A panther, even if it is only a cowardly lifter of sheep or dogs, is not to be trifled with. And this particular panther had shown some daring by seizing the dog even before it was dark.

Still, there was no question of staying away from school. If Bisnu remained at home every time a panther put in an appearance, he might just as well stop going to school altogether.

He set off even earlier than usual and reached the meeting of the paths long before Sarru. He did not wait for his friend, because he did not feel like talking about the loss of his dog. It was not the day for the postman, and so Bisnu reached Kemptee without meeting anyone on the way. He tried creeping past the hospital gate unnoticed, but Dr Taylor saw him and the first thing she said was: 'Where's Sheroo? I've got something for him.'

When Dr Taylor saw the boy's face, she knew at once that something was wrong.

'What is it, Bisnu?' she asked. She looked quickly up and down the road. 'Is it Sheroo?'

He nodded gravely.

'A panther took him,' he said.

'In the village?'

'No, while we were walking home through the forest. I did not see anything—but I heard.'

Dr Taylor knew that there was nothing she could say that would console him, and she tried to conceal the bone which she had brought out for the dog, but Bisnu noticed her hiding it behind her back and the tears welled up in his eyes. He turned away and began running down the road.

His schoolfellows noticed Sheroo's absence and questioned Bisnu. He had to tell them everything. They were full of sympathy, but they were also quite thrilled at what had happened and kept pestering Bisnu for all the details. There was a lot of noise in the classroom, and Mr Nautiyal had to call for order. When he learnt what had happened, he patted Bisnu on the head and told him that he need not attend school for the rest of the day. But Bisnu did not want to go home. After school, he got into a fight with one of the boys, and that helped him forget.

4

The panther that plunged the village into an atmosphere of gloom and terror may not have been the same panther that took Sheroo. There was no way of knowing, and it would have made no difference, because the panther that came by night and struck at the people of Manjari was that most feared of wild creatures—a man-eater.

Nine-year-old Sanjay, son of Kalam Singh, was the first child to be attacked by the panther.

Kalam Singh's house was the last in the village and nearest to the stream. Like the other houses, it was quite small, just a room above and a stable below, with steps leading up from outside the house. He lived there with his wife, two sons (Sanjay was the youngest) and little daughter Basanti, who had just turned three.

Sanjay had brought his father's cows home after grazing them on the hillside in the company of other children. He had also brought home an edible wild plant, which his mother cooked into a tasty dish for their evening meal. They had their food at dusk, sitting on the floor of their single room, and soon after, settled down for the night. Sanjay curled up in his favourite spot, with his head near the door, where he got a little fresh air. As the nights were warm, the door was usually left a little ajar. Sanjay's mother piled ash on the embers of the fire and the family was soon asleep.

No one heard the stealthy padding of a panther approaching the door, pushing it wider open. But suddenly there were sounds of a frantic struggle, and Sanjay's stifled cries were mixed with the grunts of the panther. Kalam Singh leapt to his feet with a shout. The panther had dragged Sanjay out of the door and was pulling him down the steps, when Kalam Singh started battering at the animal with a large stone. The rest of the family screamed in terror, rousing the entire village. A number of men came to Kalam Singh's assistance, and the panther was driven off. But Sanjay lay unconscious.

Someone brought a lantern and the boy's mother screamed when she saw her small son with his head lying in a pool of blood. It looked as if the side of his head had been eaten off by the panther. But he was still alive, and as Kalam Singh plastered ash on the boy's head to stop the bleeding, he found that though the scalp had been torn off one side of the head, the bare bone was smooth and unbroken.

'He won't live through the night,' said a neighbour. 'We'll have to carry him down to the river in the morning.'

The dead were always cremated on the banks of a small river which flowed past Manjari village.

Suddenly the panther, still prowling about the village, called out in rage and frustration, and the villagers rushed to their homes in panic and barricaded themselves in for the night.

Sanjay's mother sat by the boy for the rest of the night, weeping and watching. Towards dawn he started to moan and show signs of coming round. At this sign of returning consciousness, Kalam Singh rose determinedly and looked around for his stick.

He told his elder son to remain with the mother and daughter, as he was going to take Sanjay to Dr Taylor at the hospital.

'See, he is moaning and in pain,' said Kalam Singh. 'That means he has a chance to live if he can be treated at once.'

With a stout stick in his hand, and Sanjay on his back, Kalam Singh set off on the two miles of hard mountain track to the hospital at Kemptee. His son, a bloodstained cloth around his head, was moaning but still hadn't regained consciousness. When at last Kalam Singh climbed up through the last fields below the hospital, he asked for the doctor and stammered out an account of what had happened.

It was a terrible injury, as Dr Taylor discovered. The bone over almost one-third of the head was bare and the scalp was torn all round. As the father told his story, the doctor cleaned and dressed the wound, and then gave Sanjay a shot of penicillin to prevent sepsis. Later, Kalam Singh carried the boy home again.

5

After this, the panther went away for some time. But the people of Manjari could not be sure of its whereabouts. They kept to their houses after dark and shut their doors. Bisnu had to stop going to school, because there was no one to accompany him and it was dangerous to go alone. This worried him, because his final exam was only a few weeks off and he would be missing important classwork. When he wasn't in the fields, helping with the sowing of rice and maize, he would be sitting in the shade of a chestnut tree, going through his well-thumbed second-hand school books. He had no other reading, except for a copy of the Ramayana and a Hindi translation of *Alice in Wonderland*. These were well-preserved, read only in fits and starts, and usually kept locked in his mother's old tin trunk.

Sanjay had nightmares for several nights and woke up screaming. But with the resilience of youth, he quickly recovered. At the end of the week, he was able to walk to the hospital, though his father always accompanied him. Even a desperate panther will hesitate to attack a party of two. Sanjay, with his thin little face and huge bandaged head, looked a pathetic figure, but he was getting better and the wound looked healthy.

Bisnu often went to see him, and the two boys spent long hours together near the stream. Sometimes Chittru would join them, and they would try catching fish with a home-made net. They were often successful in taking home one or two mountain trout. Sometimes, Bisnu and Chittru wrestled in the shallow water or on the grassy banks of the stream. Chittru was a chubby boy with a broad chest, strong legs and thighs, and when he used his weight he got Bisnu under him. But Bisnu was hard and wiry and had very strong wrists and fingers. When he had Chittru in a vice, the bigger boy would cry out and give up the struggle. Sanjay could not join in these games. He had never been a very strong boy and he needed plenty of rest if his wounds were to heal well.

The panther had not been seen for over a week, and the people of Manjari were beginning to hope that it might have moved on over the mountain or further down the valley.

'I think I can start going to school again,' said Bisnu. 'The panther has gone away.'

'Don't be too sure,' said Puja. 'The moon is full these days and perhaps it is only being cautious.'

'Wait a few days,' said their mother. 'It is better to wait. Perhaps you could go the day after tomorrow when Sanjay goes to the hospital with his father. Then you will not be alone.'

And so, two days later, Bisnu went up to Kemptee with Sanjay and Kalam Singh. Sanjay's wound had almost healed over. Little islets of flesh had grown over the bone. Dr Taylor told him that he need come to see her only once a fortnight, instead of every third day.

Bisnu went to his school, and was given a warm welcome by his friends and by Mr Nautiyal.

'You'll have to work hard,' said his teacher. 'You have to catch up with the others. If you like, I can give you some extra time after classes.'

'Thank you, sir, but it will make me late,' said Bisnu. 'I must get home before it is dark, otherwise my mother will worry. I think the panther has gone but nothing is certain.'

'Well, you mustn't take risks. Do your best, Bisnu. Work hard and you'll soon catch up with your lessons.'

Sanjay and Kalam Singh were waiting for him outside the school. Together they took the path down to Manjari, passing the postman on the way. Mela Ram said he had heard that the panther was in another district and that there was nothing to fear. He was on his rounds again.

Nothing happened on the way. The langurs were back in their favourite part of the forest. Bisnu got home just as the kerosene lamp was being lit. Puja met him at the door with a winsome smile.

'Did you get the bangles?' she asked.

But Bisnu had forgotten again.

6

There had been a thunderstorm and some rain—a short, sharp shower which gave the villagers hope that the monsoon would arrive on time. It brought out the thunder lilies—pink, crocus-like flowers which sprang up on the hillsides immediately after a summer shower.

Bisnu, on his way home from school, was caught in the rain. He knew the shower would not last, so he took shelter in a small cave and, to pass the time, began doing sums, scratching figures in the damp earth with the end of a stick.

When the rain stopped, he came out from the cave and continued down the path. He wasn't in a hurry. The rain had made everything smell fresh and good. The scent from fallen pine needles rose from the wet earth. The leaves of the oak trees had been washed clean and a light breeze turned them about, showing their silver undersides. The birds, refreshed and high-spirited, set up a terrific noise. The worst offenders were the yellow-bottomed bulbuls who squabbled and fought in the blackberry bushes. A barbet, high up in the branches of a deodar, set up its querulous, plaintive call. And a flock of bright green parrots came swooping down the hill to settle in a wild plum tree and feast on the unripe fruit. The langurs, too, had been revived by the rain. They leapt friskily from tree to tree greeting Bisnu with little grunts.

He was almost out of the oak forest when he heard a faint bleating. Presently, a little goat came stumbling up the path towards him. The kid was far from home and must have strayed from the rest of the herd. But it was not yet conscious of being lost. It came to Bisnu with a hop, skip and a jump and started nuzzling against his legs like a cat.

'I wonder who you belong to,' mused Bisnu, stroking the little creature. 'You'd better come home with me until someone claims you.'

He didn't have to take the kid in his arms. It was used to humans and followed close at his heels. Now that darkness was coming on, Bisnu walked a little faster.

He had not gone very far when he heard the sawing grunt of a panther.

The sound came from the hill to the right, and Bisnu judged the distance to be anything from a hundred to two hundred yards. He hesitated on the path, wondering what to do. Then he picked the kid up in his arms and hurried on in the direction of home and safety.

The panther called again, much closer now. If it was an ordinary panther, it would go away on finding that the kid was with Bisnu. If it was the man-eater, it would not hesitate to attack the boy, for no man-eater fears a human. There was no time to lose and there did not seem much point in running. Bisnu looked up and down the hillside. The forest was far behind him and there were only a few trees in his vicinity. He chose a spruce.

The branches of the Himalayan spruce are very brittle and snap easily beneath a heavy weight. They were strong enough to support Bisnu's light frame. It was unlikely they would take the weight of a full-grown panther. At least that was what Bisnu hoped.

Holding the kid with one arm, Bisnu gripped a low branch

and swung himself up into the tree. He was a good climber. Slowly but confidently he climbed half-way up the tree, until he was about twelve feet above the ground. He couldn't go any higher without risking a fall.

He had barely settled himself in the crook of a branch when the panther came into the open, running into the clearing at a brisk trot. This was no stealthy approach, no wary stalking of its prey. It was the man-eater, all right. Bisnu felt a cold shiver run down his spine. He felt a little sick.

The panther stood in the clearing with a slight thrusting forward of the head. This gave it the appearance of gazing intently and rather short-sightedly at some invisible object in the clearing. But there is nothing short-sighted about a panther's vision. Its sight and hearing are acute.

Bisnu remained motionless in the tree and sent up a prayer to all the gods he could think of. But the kid began bleating. The panther looked up and gave its deep-throated, rasping grunt—a fearsome sound, calculated to strike terror in any treeborne animal. Many a monkey, petrified by a panther's roar, has fallen from its perch to make a meal for Mr Spots. The man-eater was trying the same technique on Bisnu. But though the boy was trembling with fright, he clung firmly to the base of the spruce tree.

The panther did not make any attempt to leap up the tree. Perhaps it knew instinctively that this was not the type of tree that it could climb. Instead, it described a semicircle round the tree, keeping its face turned towards Bisnu. Then it disappeared into the bushes.

The man-eater was cunning. It hoped to put the boy off

his guard, perhaps entice him down from the tree. For, a few seconds later, with a half-humorous growl, it rushed back into the clearing and then stopped, staring up at the boy in some surprise. The panther was getting frustrated. It snarled, and putting its forefeet up against the tree trunk began scratching at the bark in the manner of an ordinary domestic cat. The tree shook at each thud of the beast's paw.

Bisnu began shouting for help.

The moon had not yet come up. Down in Manjari village, Bisnu's mother and sister stood in their lighted doorway, gazing anxiously up the pathway. Every now and then, Puja would turn to take a look at the small clock.

Sanjay's father appeared in a field below. He had a kerosene lantern in his hand.

'Sister, isn't your boy home as yet?' he asked.

'No, he hasn't arrived. We are very worried. He should have been home an hour ago. Do you think the panther will be about tonight? There's going to be a moon.'

'True, but it will be dark for another hour. I will fetch the other menfolk, and we will go up the mountain for your boy. There may have been a landslide during the rain. Perhaps the path has been washed away.'

'Thank you, brother. But arm yourselves, just in case the panther is about.'

'I will take my spear,' said Kalam Singh. 'I have sworn to spear that devil when I find him. There is some evil spirit dwelling in the beast and it must be destroyed!'

'I am coming with you,' said Puja.

'No, you cannot go,' said her mother. 'It's bad enough

that Bisnu is in danger. You stay at home with me. This is work for men.'

'I shall be safe with them,' insisted Puja. 'I am going, Mother!' And she jumped down the embankment into the field and followed Sanjay's father through the village.

Ten minutes later, two men armed with axes had joined Kalam Singh in the courtyard of his house, and the small party moved silently and swiftly up the mountain path. Puja walked in the middle of the group, holding the lantern. As soon as the village lights were hidden by a shoulder of the hill, the men began to shout—both to frighten the panther, if it was about, and to give themselves courage.

Bisnu's mother closed the front door and turned to the image of Ganesha, the god for comfort and help.

Bisnu's calls were carried on the wind, and Puja and the men heard him while they were still half a mile away. Their own shouts increased in volume and, hearing their voices, Bisnu felt strength return to his shaking limbs. Emboldened by the approach of his own people, he began shouting insults at the snarling panther, then throwing twigs and small branches at the enraged animal. The kid added its bleats to the boy's shouts, and the birds took up the chorus. The langurs squealed and grunted, and the searchers shouted themselves hoarse, and the panther howled with rage. The forest had never before been so noisy.

As the search party drew near, they could hear the panther's savage snarls, and hurried, fearing that perhaps Bisnu had been seized. Puja began to run.

'Don't rush ahead, girl,' said Kalam Singh. 'Stay between us.'

The panther, now aware of the approaching humans, stood still in the middle of the clearing, head thrust forward in a familiar stance. There seemed too many men for one panther. When the animal saw the light of the lantern dancing between the trees, it turned, snarled defiance and hate, and without another look at the boy in the tree, disappeared into the bushes. It was not yet ready for a showdown.

7

Nobody turned up to claim the little goat, so Bisnu kept it. A goat was a poor substitute for a dog, but, like Mary's lamb, it followed Bisnu wherever he went, and the boy couldn't help being touched by its devotion. He took it down to the stream, where it would skip about in the shallows and nibble the sweet grass that grew on the banks.

As for the panther, frustrated in its attempt on Bisnu's life, it did not wait long before attacking another human.

It was Chittru who came running down the path one afternoon, bubbling excitedly about the panther and the postman.

Chittru, deeming it safe to gather ripe bilberries in the daytime, had walked about half a mile up the path from the village, when he had stumbled across Mela Ram's mailbag lying on the ground. Of the postman himself there was no sign. But a trail of blood led through the bushes.

Once again, a party of men headed by Kalam Singh and accompanied by Bisnu and Chittru, went out to look for the postman. But though they found Mela Ram's bloodstained clothes, they could not find his body. The panther had made no mistake this time.

It was to be several weeks before Manjari had a new postman.

A few days after Mela Ram's disappearance, an old woman was sleeping with her head near the open door of her house. She had been advised to sleep inside with the door closed, but the nights were hot and anyway the old woman was a little deaf, and in the middle of the night, an hour before moonrise, the panther seized her by the throat. Her strangled cry woke her grown-up son, and all the men in the village woke up at his shouts and came running.

The panther dragged the old woman out of the house and down the steps, but left her when the men approached with their axes and spears, and made off into the bushes. The old woman was still alive, and the men made a rough stretcher of bamboo and vines and started carrying her up the path. But they had not gone far when she began to cough, and because of her terrible throat wounds, her lungs collapsed and she died.

It was the 'dark of the month'—the week of the new moon when nights are darkest.

Bisnu, closing the front door and lighting the kerosene lantern, said, 'I wonder where that panther is tonight!'

The panther was busy in another village: Sarru's village.

A woman and her daughter had been out in the evening bedding the cattle down in the stable. The girl had gone into the house and the woman was following. As she bent down to go in at the low door, the panther sprang from the bushes.

Fortunately, one of its paws hit the doorpost and broke the force of the attack, or the woman would have been killed. When she cried out, the men came round shouting and the panther slunk off. The woman had deep scratches on her back and was badly shocked.

The next day, a small party of villagers presented themselves in front of the magistrate's office at Kemptee and demanded that something be done about the panther. But the magistrate was away on tour, and there was no one else in Kemptee who had a gun. Mr Nautiyal met the villagers and promised to write to a well-known shikari, but said that it would be at least a fortnight before the shikari would be able to come.

Bisnu was fretting because he could not go to school. Most boys would be only too happy to miss school, but when you are living in a remote village in the mountains and having an education is the only way of seeing the world, you look forward to going to school, even if it is five miles from home. Bisnu's exams were only two weeks off, and he didn't want to remain in the same class while the others were promoted. Besides, he knew he could pass even though he had missed a number of lessons. But he had to sit for the exams. He couldn't miss them.

'Cheer up, Bhaiya,' said Puja, as they sat drinking glasses of hot tea after their evening meal. 'The panther may go away once the rains break.'

'Even the rains are late this year,' said Bisnu. 'It's so hot and dry. Can't we open the door?'

'And be dragged down the steps by the panther?' said his mother. 'It isn't safe to have the window open, let alone the door.' And she went to the small window—through which a cat would have found difficulty in passing—and bolted it firmly.

With a sigh of resignation, Bisnu threw off all his clothes except his underwear and stretched himself out on the earthen floor.

'We will be rid of the beast soon,' said his mother. 'I know it in my heart. Our prayers will be heard, and you shall go to school and pass your exams.'

To cheer up her children, she told them a humorous story which had been handed down to her by her grandmother. It was all about a tiger, a panther and a bear, the three of whom were made to feel very foolish by a thief hiding in the hollow trunk of a banyan tree. Bisnu was sleepy and did not listen very attentively. He dropped off to sleep before the story was finished.

When he woke, it was dark and his mother and sister were asleep on the cot. He wondered what it was that had woken him. He could hear his sister's easy breathing and the steady ticking of the clock. Far away an owl hooted—an unlucky sign, his mother would have said; but she was asleep and Bisnu was not superstitious.

And then he heard something scratching at the door, and the hair on his head felt tight and prickly. It was like a cat scratching, only louder. The door creaked a little whenever it felt the impact of the paw—a heavy paw, as Bisnu could tell from the dull sound it made.

'It's the panther,' he muttered under his breath, sitting up on the hard floor.

The door, he felt, was strong enough to resist the panther's weight. And if he set up an alarm, he could rouse the village. But the middle of the night was no time for the bravest of men to tackle a panther.

In a corner of the room stood a long bamboo stick with a sharp knife tied to one end, which Bisnu sometimes used for spearing fish. Crawling on all fours across the room, he grasped the home-made spear, and then, scrambling on to a cupboard, he drew level with the skylight window. He could get his head and shoulders through the window.

'What are you doing up there?' said Puja, who had woken up at the sound of Bisnu shuffling about the room.

'Be quiet,' said Bisnu. 'You'll wake Mother.'

Their mother was awake by now. 'Come down from there, Bisnu. I can hear a noise outside.'

'Don't worry,' said Bisnu, who found himself looking down on the wriggling animal which was trying to get its paw in under the door. With his mother and Puja awake, there was no time to lose. He had got the spear through the window, and though he could not manoeuvre it so as to strike the panther's head, he brought the sharp end down with considerable force on the animal's rump.

With a roar of pain and rage the man-eater leapt down from the steps and disappeared into the darkness. It did not pause to see what had struck it. Certain that no human could have come upon it in that fashion, it ran fearfully to its lair, howling until the pain subsided.

8

A panther is an enigma. There are occasions when it proves itself to be the most cunning animal under the sun, and yet the very next day it will walk into an obvious trap that no self-respecting jackal would ever go near. One day a panther will prove itself to be a complete coward and run like a hare from a couple of dogs, and on the very next, it will dash in amongst half a dozen men sitting round a camp fire and inflict terrible injuries on them.

It is not often that a panther is taken by surprise, as its power of sight and hearing are very acute. It is a master at the art of camouflage, and its spotted coat is admirably suited for the purpose. It does not need heavy jungle to hide in. A couple of bushes and the light and shade from surrounding trees are enough to make it almost invisible.

Because the Manjari panther had been fooled by Bisnu, it did not mean that it was a stupid panther. It simply meant that it had been a little careless. And Bisnu and Puja, growing in confidence since their midnight encounter with the animal, became a little careless themselves.

Puja was hoeing the last field above the house and Bisnu, at the other end of the same field, was chopping up several branches of green oak, prior to leaving the wood to dry in the loft. It was late afternoon and the descending sun glinted in patches on the small river. It was a time of day when only the most desperate and daring of man-eaters would be likely to show itself.

Pausing for a moment to wipe the sweat from his brow,

Bisnu glanced up at the hillside, and his eye caught sight of a rock on the brown of the hill which seemed unfamiliar to him. Just as he was about to look elsewhere, the round rock began to grow and then alter its shape, and Bisnu, watching in fascination, was at last able to make out the head and forequarters of the panther. It looked enormous from the angle at which he saw it, and for a moment he thought it was a tiger. But Bisnu knew instinctively that it was the man-eater.

Slowly, the wary beast pulled itself to its feet and began to walk round the side of the great rock. For a second it disappeared and Bisnu wondered if it had gone away. Then it reappeared and the boy was all excitement again. Very slowly and silently the panther walked across the face of the rock until it was in direct line with the corner of the field where Puja was working.

With a thrill of horror Bisnu realized that the panther was stalking his sister. He shook himself free from the spell which had woven itself round him and shouting hoarsely ran forward.

'Run, Puja, run!' he called. 'It's on the hill above you!'

Puja turned to see what Bisnu was shouting about. She saw him gesticulate to the hill behind her, looked up just in time to see the panther crouching for his spring.

With great presence of mind, she leapt down the banking of the field and tumbled into an irrigation ditch.

The springing panther missed its prey, lost its foothold on the slippery shale banking and somersaulted into the ditch a few feet away from Puja. Before the animal could recover from its surprise, Bisnu was dashing down the slope, swinging his axe and shouting, *'Maro, maro* (Kill, kill)!'

Two men came running across the field. They, too, were armed with axes. Together with Bisnu they made a half-circle around the snarling animal, which turned at bay and plunged at them in order to get away. Puja wriggled along the ditch on her stomach. The men aimed their axes at the panther's head, and Bisnu had the satisfaction of getting in a well-aimed blow between the eyes. The animal then charged straight at one of the men, knocked him over and tried to get at his throat. Just then Sanjay's father arrived with his long spear. He plunged the end of the spear into the panther's neck.

The panther left its victim and ran into the bushes, dragging the spear through the grass and leaving a trail of blood on the ground. The men followed cautiously—all except the man who had been wounded and who lay on the ground, while Puja and the other womenfolk rushed up to help him.

The panther had made for the bed of the stream and Bisnu, Sanjay's father and their companion were able to follow it quite easily. The water was red where the panther had crossed the stream, and the rocks were stained with blood. After they had gone downstream for about a furlong, they found the panther lying still on its side at the edge of the water. It was mortally wounded, but it continued to wave its tail like an angry cat. Then, even the tail lay still.

'It is dead,' said Bisnu. 'It will not trouble us again in this body.'

'Let us be certain,' said Sanjay's father, and he bent down and pulled the panther's tail.

There was no response.

'It is dead,' said Kalam Singh. 'No panther would suffer such an insult were it alive!'

They cut down a long piece of thick bamboo and tied the panther to it by its feet. Then, with their enemy hanging upside down from the bamboo pole, they started back for the village.

'There will be a feast at my house tonight,' said Kalam Singh. 'Everyone in the village must come. And tomorrow we will visit all the villages in the valley and show them the dead panther, so that they may move about again without fear.'

'We can sell the skin in Kemptee,' said their companion. 'It will fetch a good price.'

'But the claws we will give to Bisnu,' said Kalam Singh, putting his arm around the boy's shoulders. 'He has done a man's work today. He deserves the claws.'

A panther's or tiger's claws are considered to be lucky charms.

'I will take only three claws,' said Bisnu. 'One each for my mother and sister, and one for myself. You may give the others to Sanjay and Chittru and the smaller children.'

As the sun set, a big fire was lit in the middle of the village of Manjari and the people gathered round it, singing and laughing. Kalam Singh killed his fattest goat and there was meat for everyone.

9

Bisnu was on his way home. He had just handed in his first paper, arithmetic, which he had found quite easy. Tomorrow it would be algebra, and when he got home he would have to practice square roots and cube roots and fractional coefficients.

Mr Nautiyal and the entire class had been happy that Bisnu had been able to sit for the exams. He was also a hero to them for his part in killing the panther. The story had spread through the villages with the rapidity of a forest fire, a fire which was now raging in Kemptee town.

When he walked past the hospital, he was whistling cheerfully. Dr Taylor waved to him from the veranda steps.

'How is Sanjay now?' she asked.

'He is well,' said Bisnu.

'And your mother and sister?'

'They are well,' said Bisnu.

'Are you going to get yourself a new dog?'

'I am thinking about it,' said Bisnu. 'At present I have a baby goat—I am teaching it to swim!'

He started down the path to the valley. Dark clouds had gathered and there was a rumble of thunder. A storm was imminent.

'Wait for me!' shouted Sarru, running down the path behind Bisnu, his milk cans clanging against each other. He fell into step beside Bisnu.

'Well, I hope we don't have any more man-eaters for some time,' he said. 'I've lost a lot of money by not being able to take milk up to Kemptee.'

'We should be safe as long as a shikari doesn't wound another panther. There was an old bullet wound in the man-eater's thigh. That's why it couldn't hunt in the forest. The deer were too fast for it.'

'Is there a new postman yet?'

'He starts tomorrow. A cousin of Mela Ram's.'

When they reached the parting of their ways it had begun to rain a little.

'I must hurry,' said Sarru. 'It's going to get heavier any minute.'

'I feel like getting wet,' said Bisnu. 'This time it's the monsoon, I'm sure.'

Bisnu entered the forest on his own, and at the same time the rain came down in heavy opaque sheets. The trees shook in the wind, the langurs chattered with excitement.

It was still pouring when Bisnu emerged from the forest, drenched to the skin. But the rain stopped suddenly, just as the village of Manjari came in view. The sun appeared through a rift in the clouds. The leaves and the grass gave out a sweet, fresh smell.

Bisnu could see his mother and sister in the field transplanting the rice seedlings. The menfolk were driving the yoked oxen through the thin mud of the fields, while the children hung on to the oxen's tails, standing on the plain wooden harrows and, with weird cries and shouts, sending the animals almost at a gallop along the narrow terraces.

Bisnu felt the urge to be with them, working in the fields. He ran down the path, his feet falling softly on the wet earth. Puja saw him coming and waved to him. She met him at the edge of the field.

'How did you find your paper today?' she asked.

'Oh, it was easy.' Bisnu slipped his hand into hers and together they walked across the field. Puja felt something smooth and hard against her fingers, and before she could see what Bisnu was doing, he had slipped a pair of bangles over her wrist.

'I remembered,' he said, with a sense of achievement.

Puja looked at the bangles and burst out: 'But they are blue, Bhaiya, and I wanted red and gold bangles!' And then, when she saw him looking crestfallen, she hurried on: 'But they are very pretty, and you did remember... Actually, they're just as nice as the red and gold bangles! Come into the house when you are ready. I have made something special for you.'

'I am coming,' said Bisnu, turning towards the house. 'You don't know how hungry a man gets, walking five miles to reach home!'

THE OWL

~

At night, when all is still,
The forest's sentinel
Glides silently across the hill
And perches in an old pine tree.
A friendly presence his!
No harm can come
From a night bird on the prowl.
His cry is mellow,
Much softer than a peacock's call.
Why then this fear of owls
Calling in the night?
If men must speak,
Then owls must hoot—
They have the right.
On me it casts no spell:
Rather, it seems to cry,
'The night is good—all's well, all's well.'

A CROW FOR ALL SEASONS

~

Early to bed and early to rise makes a crow healthy, wealthy and wise.

They say it's true for humans too. I'm not so sure about that. But for crows it's a must.

I'm always up at the crack of dawn, often the first crow to break the night's silence with a lusty caw. My friends and relatives, who roost in the same tree, grumble a bit and mutter to themselves, but they are soon cawing just as loudly. Long before the sun is up, we set off on the day's work.

We do not pause even for the morning wash. Later in the day, if it's hot and muggy, I might take a dip in some human's bath water; but early in the morning we like to be up and about before everyone else. This is the time when trash cans and refuse dumps are overflowing with goodies, and we like to sift through them before the dustmen arrive in their disposal trucks.

Not that we are afraid of a famine in refuse. As human beings multiply, so does their rubbish.

Only yesterday I rescued an old typewriter ribbon from the dustbin, just before it was emptied. What a waste that would have been! I had no use for it myself, but I gave it to one of my cousins who got married recently, and she tells me it's just right for her nest, the one she's building on a telegraph pole. It helps her bind the twigs together, she says.

My own preference is for toothbrushes. They're just a hobby really, like stamp-collecting with humans. I have a small but select collection which I keep in a hole in the garden wall. Don't ask me how many I've got—crows don't believe there's any point in counting beyond two—but I know there's more than *one*, that there's a whole lot of them in fact, because there isn't anyone living on this road who hasn't lost a toothbrush to me at some time or another.

We crows living in the jackfruit tree have this stretch of road to ourselves, but so that we don't quarrel or have misunderstandings we've shared the houses out. I picked the bungalow with the orchard at the back. After all, I don't eat rubbish and throwaways all the time. Just occasionally, I like a ripe guava or the soft flesh of a papaya. And sometimes I like the odd beetle as an *hors d'oeuvre*. Those humans in the bungalow should be grateful to me for keeping down the population of fruit-eating beetles, and even for recycling their refuse; but no, humans are never grateful. No sooner do I settle in one of their guava trees than stones are whizzing past me. So I return to the dustbin on the back veranda steps. They don't mind my being there.

One of my cousins shares the bungalow with me, but he's a lazy fellow and I have to do most of the foraging. Sometimes I get him to lend me a claw, but most of the time he's preening his feathers and trying to look handsome for a pretty young thing who lives in the banyan tree at the next turning.

When he's in the mood he can be invaluable, as he proved recently when I was having some difficulty getting at the dog's food on the veranda.

This dog, who is fussed over so much by the humans, I've adopted is a great big fellow, a mastiff who pretends to a pedigree going back to the time of Genghis Khan—he likes to pretend one of his ancestors was the great Khan's watchdog. But, as often happens in famous families, animal or human, there is a falling off in quality over a period of time, and this huge fellow—Tiger, they call him—is a case in point. All brawn and no brain. Many's the time I've removed a juicy bone from his plate or helped myself to pickings from under his nose.

But of late he's been growing canny and selfish. He doesn't like to share any more. And the other day I was almost in his jaws when he took a sudden lunge at me. Snap went his great teeth; but all he got was one of my tail feathers. He spat it out in disgust. Who wants crow's meat, anyway?

All the same, I thought, I'd better not be too careless. It's not for nothing that a crow's IQ is way above that of all other birds. And it's higher than a dog's, I bet.

I woke Cousin Slow from his midday siesta and said, 'Hey, Slow, we've got a problem. If you want any of that delicious tripe today, you've got to lend a claw—or a beak. That dog's getting snappier day by day.'

Slow opened one eye and said, 'Well, if you insist. But you know how I hate getting into a scuffle. It's bad for the gloss on my feathers.'

'I don't insist,' I said politely. 'But I'm not foraging for both of us today. It's every crow for himself.'

'Okay, okay, I'm coming,' said Slow, and with barely a flap he dropped down from the tree to the wall.

'What's the strategy?' I asked.

'Simple. We'll just give him the old one-two.'

We flew across to the veranda. Tiger had just started his meal. He was a fast, greedy eater who made horrible slurping sounds while he guzzled his food. We had to move fast if we wanted to get something before the meal was over.

I sidled up to Tiger and wished him good afternoon.

He kept on gobbling—but quicker now.

Slow came up from behind and gave him a quick peck near the tail—a sensitive spot—and, as Tiger swung round, snarling, I moved in quickly and snatched up several tidbits.

Tiger went for me, and I flew freestyle for the garden wall. The dish was untended, so Slow helped himself to as many scraps as he could stuff in his mouth.

He joined me on the garden wall, and we sat there feasting, while Tiger barked himself hoarse below.

'Go catch a cat,' said Slow, who is given to slang. 'You're in the wrong league, big boy.'

The great sage Pratyasataka—ever heard of him? I guess not—once said, 'Nothing can improve a crow.'

Like most human sages he wasn't very clear in his thinking, so that there has been some misunderstanding about what he meant. Humans like to think that what he really meant was that crows were so bad as to be beyond improvement. But we crows know better. We interpret the saying as meaning that the crow is so perfect that no improvement is possible.

It's not that we aren't human—what I mean is, there are times when we fall from our high standards and do rather foolish things. Like at lunchtime the other day.

Sometimes, when the table is laid in the bungalow, and before the family enters the dining room, I nip in through the open window and make a quick foray among the dishes. Sometimes I'm lucky enough to pick up a sausage or a slice of toast, or even a pat of butter, making off before someone enters and throws a bread knife at me. But on this occasion, just as I was reaching for the toast, a thin slouching fellow—Junior Sahib they call him—entered suddenly and shouted at me. I was so startled that I leapt across the table seeking shelter. Something flew at me, and in an effort to dodge the missile, I put my head through a circular object and then found it wouldn't come off.

It wasn't safe to hang around there, so I flew out the window with this dashed ring still round my neck.

Serviette or napkin rings, that's what they are called. Quite unnecessary objects, but some humans—particularly the well-to-do sort—seem to like having them on their tables, holding bits of cloth in place. The cloth is used for wiping the mouth. Have you ever heard of such nonsense?

Anyway, there I was with a fat napkin ring round my

neck, and as I perched on the wall trying to get it off, the entire human family gathered on their veranda to watch me.

There was the Colonel Sahib and his wife, the Memsahib; there was the scrawny Junior Sahib (worst of the lot); there was a mischievous boy (the Colonel Sahib's grandson) known as the Baba; there was the cook (who usually flung orange peels at me) and the gardener (who once tried to decapitate me with a spade), and the dog Tiger who, like most dogs, tries unsuccessfully to be human.

Today they weren't cursing and shaking their fists at me; they were just standing and laughing their heads off. What's so funny about a crow with its head stuck in a napkin ring?

Worse was to follow.

The noise had attracted the other crows in the area, and if there's one thing crows detest, it's a crow who doesn't look like a crow.

They swooped low and dived on me, hammering at the wretched napkin ring, until they had knocked me off the wall and into a flower bed. Then six or seven toughs landed on me with every intention of finishing me off.

'Hey, boys!' I cawed. 'This is me, Speedy! What are you trying to do—kill me?'

'That's right! You don't look like Speedy to us. What have you done with him, eh?'

And they set upon me with even greater vigour.

'You're just like a bunch of lousy humans!' I shouted. 'You're no better than them—this is just the way they carry on amongst themselves!'

That brought them to a halt. They stopped trying to peck

me to pieces, and stood back, looking puzzled. The napkin ring had been shattered in the onslaught and had fallen to the ground.

'Why, it's Speedy!' said one of the gang.

'None other!'

'Good old Speedy—what are you doing here? And where's the guy we were hammering just now?'

There was no point in trying to explain things to them. Crows are like that. They're all good pals—until one of them tries to look different. Then he could be just another bird.

'He took off for Tibet,' I said. 'It was getting unhealthy for him around here.'

~

Summertime is here again. And although I'm a crow for all seasons, I must admit to a preference for the summer months.

Humans grow lazy and don't pursue me with so much vigour. Garbage cans overflow. Food goes bad and is constantly being thrown away. Overripe fruit gets tastier by the minute. If fellows like me weren't around to mop up all these unappreciated riches, how would humans manage?

There's one character in the bungalow, Junior Sahib, who will never appreciate our services, it seems. He simply hates crows. The small boy may throw stones at us occasionally, but then, he's the sort who throws stones at almost anything. There's nothing personal about it. He just throws stones on principle.

The Memsahib is probably the best of the lot. She often throws me scraps from the kitchen—onion skins, potato peels, crusts, and leftovers—and even when I nip in and make off with something not meant for me (like a jam tart or a cheese pakora) she is quite sporting about it. The Junior Sahib looks outraged, but the lady of the house says, 'Well, we've all got to make a living somehow, and that's how crows make theirs. It's high time you thought of earning a living.' Junior Sahib's her nephew—that's his occupation. He has never been known to work.

The Colonel Sahib has a sense of humour but it's often directed at me. He thinks I'm a comedian.

He discovered I'd been making off with the occasional egg from the egg basket on the veranda, and one day, without my knowledge, he made a substitution.

Right on top of the pile I found a smooth round egg, and before anyone could shout, 'Crow!' I'd made off with it. It was abnormally light. I put it down on the lawn and set about cracking it with my strong beak, but it would keep slipping away or bounding off into the bushes. Finally, I got it between my feet and gave it a good hard whack. It burst open, and to my utter astonishment, there was nothing inside!

I looked up and saw the old man standing on the veranda, doubled up with laughter.

'What are you laughing at?' asked the Memsahib, coming out to see what it was all about.

'It's that ridiculous crow!' guffawed the Colonel, pointing at me. 'You know he's been stealing our eggs. Well, I placed a ping pong ball on top of the pile, and he fell for it! He's been struggling with that ball for twenty minutes! That will teach him a lesson.'

It did. But I had my revenge later, when I pinched a brand new toothbrush from the Colonel's bathroom.

The Junior Sahib has no sense of humour at all. He idles about the house and grounds all day, whistling or singing to himself.

'Even that crow sings better than Uncle,' said the boy.

A truthful boy; but all he got for his honesty was a whack on the head from his uncle.

Anyway, as a gesture of appreciation, I perched on the garden wall and gave the family a rendering of my favourite crow song, which is my own composition. Here it is, translated for your benefit:

> *Oh, for the life of a crow!*
> *A bird who's in the know.*
> *Although we are cursed,*
> *We are never dispersed—*
> *We're always on the go!*
> *I know I'm a bit of a rogue*
> *(And my voice wouldn't pass for a brogue),*
> *But there's no one as sleek*
> *Or as neat with his beak—*
> *So they're putting my picture in* Vogue!
> *Oh, for the life of a crow!*
> *I reap what I never sow,*
> *They call me a thief,*
> *Pray I'll soon come to grief—*
> *But there's no getting rid of a crow!*

I gave it everything I had, and the humans—all of them

on the lawn to enjoy the evening breeze, listened to me in silence, struck with wonder at my performance.

When I had finished, I bowed and preened myself, waiting for the applause.

They stared at each other for a few seconds. Then the Junior Sahib stooped, picked up a bottle opener, and flung it at me.

Well, I ask you!

What can one say about humans? I do my best to defend them from all kinds of criticism, and this is what I get for my pains.

Anyway, I picked up the bottle opener and added it to my collection of odds and ends.

It was getting dark, and soon everyone was stumbling around, looking for another bottle opener. Junior Sahib's popularity was even lower than mine.

One day, Junior Sahib came home carrying a heavy shotgun. He pointed it at me a few times and I dived for cover. But he didn't fire. Probably I was out of range.

'He's only threatening you,' said Slow from the safety of the jamun tree, where he sat in the shadows. 'He probably doesn't know how to fire the thing.'

But I wasn't taking any chances. I'd seen a sly look on Junior Sahib's face, and I decided that he was trying to make me careless. So I stayed well out of range.

Then one evening, I received a visit from my cousin, Charm. He'd come to me for a loan. He wanted some new bottle tops for his collection and had brought me a mouldy old toothbrush to offer in exchange.

Charm landed on the garden wall, toothbrush in his break, and was waiting for me to join him there, when there was a flash and a tremendous bang. Charm was sent several feet into the air, and landed limp and dead in a flower bed.

'I've got him, I've got him!' shouted Junior Sahib. 'I've shot that blasted crow!'

Throwing away the gun, Junior Sahib ran out into the garden, overcome with joy. He picked up my fallen relative, and began running around the bungalow with his trophy.

The rest of the family had collected on the veranda.

'Drop that thing at once!' called the Memsahib.

'Uncle is doing a war dance,' observed the boy.

'It's unlucky to shoot a crow,' said the Colonel.

I thought it was time to take a hand in the proceedings and let everyone know that the *right* crow—the one and only Speedy—was alive and kicking. So I swooped down the jackfruit tree, dived through Junior Sahib's window, and emerged with one of his socks.

Triumphantly flaunting his dead crow, Junior Sahib came dancing up the garden path, then stopped dead when he saw me perched on the window sill, a sock in my beak. His jaw fell, his eyes bulged; he looked like the owl in the banyan tree.

'You shot the wrong crow!' shouted the Colonel, and everyone roared with laughter.

Before Junior Sahib could recover from the shock, I took off in a leisurely fashion and joined Slow on the wall.

Junior Sahib came rushing out with the gun, but by now it was too dark to see anything, and I heard the Memsahib telling the Colonel, 'You'd better take that gun away before he does himself a mischief.' So the Colonel took Junior Sahib indoors and gave him a brandy.

I composed a new song for Junior Sahib's benefit, and sang it to him outside his window early next morning:

> I understand you want a crow
> To poison, shoot or smother;
> My fond salaams, but by your leave
> I'll substitute another;
> Allow me then, to introduce
> My most respected brother.

Although I was quite understanding about the whole tragic mix-up—I was, after all, the family's very own house crow—my fellow crows were outraged at what had happened to Charm, and swore vengeance on Junior Sahib.

'Corvus splendens!' they shouted with great spirit, forgetting that this title had been bestowed on us by a human. In times of war, we forget how much we owe to our enemies.

Junior Sahib had only to step into the garden, and several crows would swoop down on him, screeching and swearing and aiming lusty blows at his head and hands. He took to coming out wearing a sola topi, and even then they knocked it off and drove him indoors. Once he tried lighting a cigarette on the veranda steps, when Slow swooped low across the porch and snatched it from his lips.

Junior Sahib shut himself up in his room, and smoked countless cigarettes—a sure sign that his nerves were going to pieces.

Every now and then, the Memsahib would come out and

shoo us off; and because she wasn't an enemy, we obliged by retreating to the garden wall. After all, Slow and I depended on her for much of our board if not for our lodging. But Junior Sahib had only to show his face outside the house, and all the crows in the area would be after him like avenging furies.

'It doesn't look as though they are going to forgive you,' said the Memsahib.

'Elephants never forget, and crows never forgive,' said the Colonel.

'Would you like to borrow my catapult, Uncle?' asked the boy. 'Just for self-protection, you know.'

'Shut up,' said Junior Sahib and went to bed.

One day, he sneaked out of the back door and dashed across to the garage. A little later the family's old car, seldom used, came out of the garage with Junior Sahib at the wheel. He'd decided that if he couldn't take a walk in safety he'd go for a drive. All the windows were up.

No sooner had the car turned into the driveway than about a dozen crows dived down on it, crowding the bonnet and flapping in front of the windscreen. Junior Sahib couldn't see a thing. He swung the steering wheel left, right and centre, and the car went off the driveway, ripped through a hedge, crushed a bed of sweetpeas and came to a stop against the trunk of a mango tree.

Junior Sahib just sat there, afraid to open the door. The family had to come out of the house and rescue him.

'Are you all right?' asked the Colonel.

'I've bruised my knees,' said Junior Sahib.

'Never mind your knees,' said the Memsahib, gazing

around at the ruin of her garden. 'What about my sweetpeas?'

'I think your uncle is going to have a nervous breakdown,' I heard the Colonel saying to the boy.

'What's that?' asked the boy. 'Is it the same as a car having a breakdown?'

'Well, not exactly… But you could call it a mind breaking down.'

Junior Sahib had been refusing to leave his room or take his meals. The family was worried about him. I was worried, too. Believe it or not, we crows are among the very few birds who sincerely desire the preservation of the human species.

'He needs a change,' said the Memsahib.

'A rest cure,' said the Colonel sarcastically. 'A rest from doing nothing.'

'Send him to Switzerland,' suggested the boy.

'We can't afford that. But we can take him up to a hill station.'

The nearest hill station was some fifty miles as the human drives (only ten as the crow flies). Many people went up there during the summer months. It wasn't fancied much by crows. For one thing, it was a tidy sort of place, and people lived in houses that were set fairly far apart. Opportunities for scavenging were limited. Also it was rather cold and the trees were inconvenient and uncomfortable. A friend of mine, who had spent a night in a pine tree, said he hadn't been able to sleep because of the prickly pine needles and the wind howling through the branches.

'Let's all go up for a holiday,' said the Memsahib. 'We can spend a week in a boarding house. All of us need a change.'

A few days later the house was locked up, and the family piled into the old car and drove off to the hills.

I had the grounds to myself.

The dog had gone too, and the gardener spent all day dozing in his hammock. There was no one around to trouble me.

'We've got the whole place to ourselves,' I told Slow.

'Yes, but what good is that? With everyone gone, there are no throwaways, giveaways and takeaways!'

'We'll have to try the house next door.'

'And be driven off by the other crows? That's not our territory, you know. We can go across to help them, or to ask for their help, but we're not supposed to take their pickings. It just isn't cricket, old boy.'

We could have tried the bazaar or the railway station, where there is always a lot of rubbish to be found, but there is also a lot of competition in those places. The station crows are gangsters. The bazaar crows are bullies. Slow and I had grown soft. We'd have been no match for the bad boys.

'I've just realized how much we depend on humans,' I said.

'We could go back to living in the jungle,' said Slow.

'No, that would be too much like hard work. We'd be living on wild fruit most of the time. Besides, the jungle crows won't have anything to do with us now. Ever since we took up with humans, we became the outcasts of the bird world.'

'That means we're almost human.'

'You might say we have all their vices and none of their virtues.'

'Just a different set of values, old boy.'

'Like eating hens' eggs instead of crows' eggs. That's something in their favour. And while you're hanging around here waiting for the mangoes to fall, I'm off to locate our humans.'

Slow's beak fell open. He looked like—well, a hungry crow.

'Don't tell me you're going to follow them up to the hill station? You don't even know where they are staying.'

'I'll soon find out,' I said, and took off for the hills.

You'd be surprised at how simple it is to be a good detective, if only you put your mind to it. Of course, if Ellery Queen had been able to fly, he wouldn't have required fifteen chapters and his father's assistance to crack a case.

Swooping low over the hill station, it wasn't long before I spotted my humans' old car. It was parked outside a boarding house called Climber's Rest. I hadn't seen anyone climbing, but dozing in an armchair in the garden was my favourite human.

I perched on top of a colourful umbrella and waited for Junior Sahib to wake up. I decided it would be rather inconsiderate of me to disturb his sleep, so I waited patiently on the brolly, looking at him with one eye and keeping one eye on the house. He stirred uneasily, as though he'd suddenly had a bad dream; then he opened his eyes. I must have been the first thing he saw.

'Good morning,' I cawed in a friendly tone—always ready to forgive and forget, that's Speedy!

He leapt out of the armchair and ran into the house, hollering at the top of his voice.

I supposed he hadn't been able to contain his delight at

seeing me again. Humans can be funny that way. They'll hate you one day and love you the next.

Well, Junior Sahib ran all over the boarding house screaming: 'It's that crow, it's that crow! He's following me everywhere!'

Various people, including the family, ran outside to see what the commotion was about, and I thought it would be better to make myself scarce. So I flew to the top of a spruce tree and stayed very still and quiet.

'Crow! What crow?' said the Colonel.

'Our crow!' cried Junior Sahib. 'The one that persecutes me. I was dreaming of it just now, and when I opened my eyes, there it was, on the garden umbrella!'

'There's nothing there now,' said the Memsahib. 'You probably hadn't woken up completely.'

'He is having illusions again,' said the boy.

'Delusions,' corrected the Colonel.

'Now look here,' said the Memsahib, 'you'll have to pull yourself together. You'll take leave of your senses if you don't.'

'I tell you, it's here!' sobbed Junior Sahib. 'It's following me everywhere.'

'It's grown fond of Uncle,' said the boy. 'And it seems Uncle can't live without crows.'

Junior Sahib looked up with a wild glint in his eye.

'That's it!' he cried. 'I can't live without them. That's the answer to my problem. I don't hate crows—I love them!'

Everyone just stood around goggling at Junior Sahib.

'I'm feeling fine now,' he carried on. 'What a difference it makes if you can just do the opposite of what you've been doing before! I thought I hated crows. But all the time I really loved them!' And flapping his arms, and trying to caw like a crow, he went prancing about the garden.

'Now he thinks he's a crow,' said the boy. 'Is he still having delusions?'

'That's right,' said the Memsahib. 'Delusions of grandeur.'

After that, the family decided that there was no point in staying on in the hill station any longer. Junior Sahib had completed his rest cure. And even if he was the only one who believed himself cured, that was all right, because after all he was the one who mattered... If you're feeling fine, can there be anything wrong with you?

No sooner was everyone back in the bungalow than Junior Sahib took to hopping barefoot on the grass early every morning, all the time scattering food about for the crows. Bread, chappattis, cooked rice, curried eggplants, the Memsahib's homemade toffee—you name it, we got it!

Slow and I were the first to help ourselves to these dawn offerings, and soon the other crows had joined us on the lawn. We didn't mind. Junior Sahib brought enough for everyone.

'We ought to honour him in some way,' said Slow.

'Yes, why not?' said I. 'There was someone else, hundreds of years ago, who fed the birds. They followed him wherever he went.'

'That's right. They made him a saint. But as far as I know, he didn't feed any crows. At least, you don't see any crows in the pictures—just sparrows and robins and wagtails.'

'Small fry. *Our* human is dedicated exclusively to crows. Do you realize that, Slow?'

'Sure. We ought to make him the patron saint of crows. What do you say, fellows?'

'Caw, caw, caw!' All the crows were in agreement.

'St Corvus!' said Slow as Junior Sahib emerged from the house, laden with good things to eat.

'Corvus, corvus, corvus!' we cried.

And what a pretty picture he made—a crow eating from his hand, another perched on his shoulder, and about a dozen of us on the grass, forming a respectful ring around him.

From persecutor to protector; from beastliness to saintliness. And sometimes it can be the other way round: you never know with humans!

COPPERFIELD IN THE JUNGLE

~

Grandfather never hunted wild animals; he could not understand the pleasure some people obtained from killing the creatures of our forests. Birds and animals, he felt, had as much right to live as humans. There was some justification in killing for food—most animals did—but none at all in killing just for the fun of it.

At the age of twelve, I did not have the same high principles as Grandfather. Nevertheless, I disliked anything to do with shikar or hunting. I found it terribly boring.

Uncle Henry and some of his sporting friends once took me on a shikar expedition into the Terai forests of the Siwaliks. The prospect of a whole week in the jungle as camp follower to several adults with guns filled me with dismay. I knew that long, weary hours would be spent tramping behind these tall, professional-looking huntsmen. They could only speak in terms of bagging this tiger or that wild elephant, when all they ever got, if they were lucky, was a wild hare or a partridge. Tigers and excitement, it seemed, came only to Jim Corbett.

This particular expedition proved to be different from others. There were four men with guns, and at the end of the week, all that they had shot were two miserable, underweight wild fowls. But I managed, on our second day in the jungle, to be left behind at the rest house. And, in the course of a morning's exploration of the old bungalow, I discovered a shelf of books half-hidden in a corner of the back veranda.

Who had left them there? A literary forest officer? A memsahib who had been bored by her husband's camp-fire boasting? Or someone who had no interest in the 'manly' sport of slaughtering wild animals and had brought his library along to pass the time?

Or possibly the poor fellow had gone into the jungle one day, as a gesture towards his more bloodthirsty companions, and been trampled by an elephant, or gored by a wild boar, or (more likely) accidentally shot by one of the shikaris and his sorrowing friends had taken his remains away and left his books behind.

Anyway, there they were—a shelf of some thirty volumes, obviously untouched for many years. I wiped the thick dust off the covers and examined the titles. As my reading tastes had not yet formed, I was willing to try anything. The bookshelf was varied in its contents—and my own interests have since remained fairly universal.

On that fateful day in the forest rest house, I discovered P. G. Wodehouse and read his *Love Among the Chickens*, an early Ukridge story and still one of my favourites. By the time the perspiring hunters came home late in the evening, with their spent cartridges and lame excuses, I had made a start with M.R. James's *Ghost Stories of an Antiquary*, which had me hooked on ghost stories for the rest of my life. It kept me awake most of the night, until the oil in the kerosene lamp had finished.

Next morning, fresh and optimistic again, the shikaris set out for a different area, where they hoped to 'bag a tiger'. They had employed a party of villagers to beat the jungle, and all day I could hear their drums throbbing in the distance. This did not prevent me from finishing M.R. James or discovering a book called *A Naturalist on the Prowl* by Edward Hamilton Aitken.

My concentration was disturbed only once, when I looked up and saw a spotted deer crossing the open clearing in front of the bungalow. The deer disappeared among the sal trees, and I returned to my book.

Dusk had fallen when I heard the party returning from the hunt. The great men were talking loudly and seemed excited. Perhaps they had got their tiger. I put down my book and came out to meet them.

'Did you shoot the tiger?' I asked excitedly.

'No, my boy,' said Uncle Henry. 'I think we'll bag it tomorrow. But you should have been with us—we saw a spotted deer!'

~

There were three days left and I knew I would never get through the entire bookshelf. So I chose *David Copperfield—*

my first encounter with Dickens—and settled down on the veranda armchair to make the acquaintance of Mr Micawber and his family, Aunt Betsy Trotwood, Mr Dick, Peggotty, and a host of other larger-than-life people. I think it would be true to say that *David Copperfield* set me off on the road to literature; I identified with young David and wanted to grow up to be a writer like him.

But on my second day with the book an event occurred which disturbed my reading for a little while.

I had noticed, on the previous day, that a number of stray dogs—belonging to watchmen, villagers and forest guards—always hung about the house, waiting for scraps of food to be thrown away. It was ten o'clock in the morning, a time when wild animals seldom come into the open, when I heard a sudden yelp in the clearing. Looking up, I saw a large leopard making off into the jungle with one of the dogs held in its jaws. The leopard had either been driven towards the house by the beaters, or had watched the party leave the bungalow and decided to help itself to a meal.

There was no one else about at the time. Since the dog was obviously dead within seconds of being seized, and the leopard had disappeared, I saw no point in raising an alarm which would have interrupted my reading. So I returned to *David Copperfield*.

It was getting late when the shikaris returned. They were dirty, sweaty, and as usual, disappointed. Next day we were to return to the city, and none of the hunters had anything to show for a week in the jungle. Swear words punctuated their conversation.

'No game left in these… jungles,' said the leading member of the party, famed for once having shot two man-eating tigers and a basking crocodile in rapid succession.

'It's this beastly weather,' said Uncle Henry. 'No rain for months.'

'I saw a leopard this morning,' I said modestly.

But no one took me seriously. 'Did you really?' said the leading hunter, glancing at the book beside me. 'Young Master Copperfield says he saw a leopard!'

'Too imaginative for his age,' said Uncle Henry. 'Comes from reading too much, I suppose.'

'If you were to get out of the house and into the jungle,' said the third member, 'you might really see a leopard! Don't know what young chaps are coming to these days.'

I went to bed early and left them to their tales of the 'good old days' when rhinos, cheetahs, and possibly even the legendary phoenix were still available for slaughter.

Next day the camp broke up and we went our different ways. I was still only half-way through *David Copperfield*, but I saw no reason why it should be left behind to gather dust for another thirty years, and so I took it home with me. I have it still, a reminder of how I failed as a shikari but launched myself on a literary career.

AN ISLAND OF TREES

~

Koki and her grandmother were sitting on a string cot in the shade of an old jackfruit tree, and Grandmother was talking about her father and his great love for trees and flowers.

Grandmother said, 'I was never able to get over the feeling that plants and trees loved my father with as much tenderness as he loved them. I was sitting beside him on the veranda steps one morning, when I noticed the tendril of a creeping vine that was trailing near my feet. As we sat there in the soft winter sunshine, I saw the tendril moving very slowly away from me and towards my father. Twenty minutes later, it had crossed the veranda steps and was touching my father's feet.

'There is probably a scientific explanation for the plant's behaviour—something to do with light and warmth—but I like to think that it moved simply because it was fond of my father.

'One felt like drawing close to him. Sometimes when I sat alone beneath a tree, I would feel a little lonely or lost. But as soon as my father joined me, the garden would become a happy place, the tree itself more friendly.

'Your great-grandfather had served many years in the Indian Forest Service and so it was natural that he should know, understand and like trees. On his retirement he built this bungalow on the outskirts of the town, planting the trees that you see around it now: limes, mangoes, oranges and guavas; also jacaranda and laburnum and the Persian lilac. In our valley, given the chance, plants and trees grow tall and strong.

'Of course there were other trees here before the house was built, including an old peepul which had forced its way through the walls of an old, abandoned temple, knocking the bricks down with its vigorous growth. Peepul trees are great show-offs. Even when there is no breeze, their broad-chested, slim-waisted leaves will spin like tops, determined to attract your attention and invite you into the shade.'

'What happened to the temple?' asked Koki.

'Well, my mother wanted the peepul tree cut down, but my father said he would save both the tree and the temple. So he rebuilt the temple around the tree, and there it is, on the other side of the wall. The tree protects the temple, and the temple protects the tree. People from these parts feel there's a friendly tree spirit dwelling there, and they bring offerings of flowers and leave them at the base of the tree.

'Did you know that I used to climb trees when I was a girl? This jackfruit was my favourite tree, it's quite easy to climb. You climb it too, don't you?

'Another good tree was the banyan behind the house. Its spreading branches, which hung to the ground and took root again, formed a number of twisting passageways. The tree was older than the house, older than my grandparents. I could hide in its branches, behind a screen of thick green leaves, and spy on the world below.

'Yes, the banyan tree was a world in itself, populated with small animals and large insects. While the leaves were still pink and tender, they would be visited by the delicate map butterfly, who left her eggs to their care.

'The "honey" on the leaves—a sweet, sticky smear—also attracted the Utile striped squirrels, who soon grew used to having me in the tree. They became quite bold, accepting food from my hand.

'At night the tree was visited by the hawk-cuckoo. Its shrill nagging cry kept us awake on hot summer nights. We call the bird "papiha", which means "rain is coming!" But, Father said that according to Englishmen living in India, it seemed to be shouting up and up the scale: "Oh dear, oh dear! How very hot it's getting! We feel it...we feel it...we feel it!"

'Well, the banyan has long since gone. It came down in a storm, aerial roots and all. Father planted another, but as you can see, it's still quite a young tree. The banyan takes a long time to grow.

'Your great-grandfather wasn't content with planting trees in the garden or near the house. During the monsoons he would walk into the scrubland and beyond the riverbed, armed with cuttings and saplings, and he would plant them out there, hoping to create a forest. But grazing cattle always finished them off.

'"No one ever goes there," I said. "Who will see your forest?"

'"We are not planting it for people to see," said my father. "We are planting it for the earth—and for the birds and animals who live on it and need more food and shelter."

'Father told me why mankind, and not only wild creatures, need trees—for keeping the desert away, for attracting rain, for preventing the banks of rivers from being washed away. But everywhere people are cutting down trees without planting new ones. If this continues, then one day there will be no forests at all and the world will become one great desert!

'The thought of a world without trees became a sort of nightmare for me. It's one reason why I shall never want to live on a treeless moon! I helped my father in his tree-planting with even greater enthusiasm.

'"One day the trees will move again," he said. "They have been standing still for thousands of years, but one day they will move again. There was a time when trees could walk about like people. Then, along came a terrible demon and cast a spell over them, rooting them to one place. But they are always trying to move—see how they reach out with their arms!"

'On one of our walks along the river bank about a mile upstream from here, we found an island, a small rocky island in the middle of the riverbed. You know what this riverbed is like—dry during summers but flooded during the monsoons. A young tamarind tree was growing in the middle of the island, and my father said, "If a tamarind can grow here, so can other trees."

'As soon as the monsoon arrived—and while the river could still be crossed—we set out with a number of mango, laburnum, hibiscus and coral tree saplings and cuttings, and spent the better part of a day planting them on the little island. We made one more visit to the island before the monsoon finally set in. Most of the plants looked quite healthy.

'The monsoon season is the best time for rambling about. At every turn there is something new to see. Out of earth and rock and leafless bough, the magic touch of the summer rain brings forth new life and verdure. You can almost see the broad-leaved vines growing. Plants spring up in the most unlikely places. A peepul took root on the roof; a mango sprouted on the windowsill. My father and I did not want to remove them, but they had to go if the house was to be prevented from falling down!

"If you two want to live in a tree, that's all right by me," said my mother. "But I like having a roof over my head, and I'm not going to have it brought down by a hanging forest. Already I can see roots breaking in through the ceiling!"

'The visiting trees were carefully removed and transplanted in the garden. Whenever we came indoors from our gardening and sat down to a meal, a ladybird or a caterpillar would invariably walk off our sleeves and wander about the kitchen, much to my mother's annoyance.

'There were flowers in the garden, too; my mother loved fragrant flowers, like roses and sweet peas and jasmine and queen of the night. But my father and I found trees more exciting. They kept growing and changing and attracting birds and other visitors.

'The banyan tree really came to life during the monsoon. The branches were thick with scarlet figs. We couldn't eat the berries, but the many birds that gathered in the tree— gossipy rosy pastors, quarrelsome mynas, cheerful bulbuls and coppersmiths, and sometimes a noisy, bullying crow—would feast on them. And when night fell and the birds were resting, the dark flying foxes flapped heavily about the tree, chewing and munching loudly as they clambered over the branches.

'The tree crickets were a band of willing artists who would start singing at almost any time of the day. At the height of the monsoon, the banyan tree was like an orchestra with the musicians constantly tuning up. A small flute in my hand, I would add my shrill piping to that of the crickets and cicadas. But they must have thought poorly of my piping because whenever I played, the insects fell silent!

'When I grew up, I was married and went to live with your grandfather in Bombay. We were there for many years, and I could only visit my parents here once or twice in all that time. I had no brothers, so when my parents died, they left the house to me. It will be yours one day. Would you rather live here or in that poky little house in the town?'

'Here,' said Koki. 'But only if you are here too, Grandmother.'

'The trees will be here,' said Grandmother.

'And what about the island?' asked Koki. 'The trees you planted with your father—are they still there?'

'You can see them for yourself if you feel like a walk. But I'll tell you what I found when I came to live here again after twenty years or more. I walked out of the old house and took the same path that my father and I used to take during our walks.

'It was February, I remember, and as I looked across the dry riverbed, my eye was immediately caught by the spectacular red plumes of the coral blossom. In contrast with the dry riverbed, the island was a small green paradise. When I walked over to the trees, I noticed that a number of parrots had come to live in them. A small spotted deer scampered away to hide in a thicket. And a wild pheasant challenged me with a mellow "who-are-you, who-are-you?"

'But the trees seemed to know me. I am sure they whispered among themselves and beckoned me nearer.

'I ran my hands over their barks and it was like touching the hands of old friends. And looking around, I noticed that other small trees and wild plants and grasses had sprung up under the protection of those whom we had planted there.

'The trees had multiplied! The forest was on the move! In one small corner of the world, my father's dream was coming true, and trees were walking again!'

'GOOD SHOT, MEHMOUD!'

~

It was a long, hot summer that year, but a summer in the plains has its compensations—such as mangoes and melons and lychees and custard apples. The fruit seller came to our house every day, a basket of fresh fruit balanced on his head. One morning, I entered the kitchen to find a bucket full of mangoes, and Mehmoud busy making a large jug of mango milkshake.

'Pass me some ice, baba, you'll find it in the bucket. You can have a milkshake now, and another with your lunch. Carpet-sahib thought highly of my milkshakes. During the mango season, he'd have two glasses of mango milkshake first thing in the morning, and then he'd go out and shoot a tiger!'

'Did *you* ever shoot a tiger?' I asked, accepting a glass from Mehmoud and adding a chunk of ice to the milkshake.

'I shot a leopard once,' said Mehmoud. 'I wasn't supposed to touch the guns, but one morning, after his milkshake,

Carpet-sahib said I could accompany him into the jungle, provided I brought along a large thermos full of mango milkshake. It was a hot, humid morning and Carpet-sahib was soon feeling thirsty.

"Hold my rifle, Mehmoud, while I have a drink," he said, and he handed me his gun and took the thermos. While he was quenching his thirst, a kakar—a barking deer—appeared in the open, just fifteen to twenty feet in front of us. 'Shall I shoot it, sir?" I asked. I'd seen him shooting many times, and I knew how the rifle worked. "Go ahead, old chap," he said. "Let's have some venison for dinner."

'So I put the rifle to my shoulder, took aim, and fired. It was the first time I'd fired a gun, and the butt sprang back and hit me in the shoulder, while the bullet itself whizzed over the deer and into the tree beneath which it was standing.

'Away went the kakar, while I held my shoulder in agony. I'd missed it by several feet. But then there was a terrible groan from the branches of the tree, and a huge leopard came crashing through the foliage, falling with a thud at our feet. It was quite dead, baba.

'I'd missed the kakar and shot a leopard. It must have been watching the deer, waiting to pounce on it, when it was struck by my bullet.

'"Good shot!" cried Carpet-sahib. 'Well aimed, Mehmoud, I didn't see the leopard.'

'"Nor did I, sir," I said.

'"But you shot it all the same," said Carpet-sahib.

'And since I did not want the skin, he rewarded me with five hundred rupees. The leopard was stuffed and kept in his veranda, to scare away the monkeys. Of course he told everyone what a good shot I was, although it was the last time he asked me to hold his gun.'

'Never mind,' I said. 'You shot the leopard, and you saved the life of the pretty deer. And your mango milkshake is the best in the world.'

'Thank you, baba,' said Mehmoud, refilling my glass. 'This is a good year for mangoes.'

And it was a good year for mango milkshakes. As I discovered.

THE SNAKE

~

When, after days of rain,
The sun appears,
The snake emerges,
Green-gold on the grass.
Kept in so long,
He basks for hours,
Soaks up the hot bright sun.
Knowing how shy he is of me,
I walk a gentle pace,
Letting him doze in peace.
But to the snake, earth-bound,
Each step must sound like thunder.
He glides away,
Goes underground.
I've known him for some years:
A harmless green grass-snake,
Who, when he sees me on the path,
Uncoils and disappears.

THE ELEPHANT AND
THE CASSOWARY BIRD

~

The baby elephant wasn't out of place in our home in North India because India is where elephants belong, and in any case, our house was full of pets brought home by Grandfather, who was in the Forest Service. But the cassowary bird was different. No one had ever seen such a bird before—not in India, that is. Grandfather had picked it up on a voyage to Singapore, where he'd been given the bird by a rubber planter who'd got it from a Dutch trader who'd got it from a man in Indonesia.

Anyway, it ended up at our home in Dehra, and seemed to do quite well in the subtropical climate. It looked like a cross between a turkey and an ostrich, but bigger than the former and smaller than the latter—about five feet in height. It was not a beautiful bird, nor even a friendly one, but it had come to stay, and everyone was curious about it, especially the baby elephant.

Right from the start, the baby elephant took a great interest in the cassowary, a bird unlike any found in the Indian jungles. He would circle round the odd creature, and diffidently examine with his trunk the texture of its stumpy wings. Of course he suspected no evil, and his childlike curiosity encouraged him to take liberties which resulted in an unpleasant experience.

Noticing the baby elephant's attempts to make friends with the rather morose cassowary, we felt a bit apprehensive. Self-contained and sullen, the big bird responded only by slowly and slyly raising one of its powerful legs, in the meantime gazing into space with an innocent air. We knew what the gesture meant; we had seen that treacherous leg raised on many an occasion, and suddenly shooting out with a force that would have done credit to a vicious camel. In fact, camel and cassowary kicks are delivered on the same plan, except that the camel kicks backward like a horse and the bird forward.

We wished to spare our baby elephant a painful experience, and led him away from the bird. But he persisted in his friendly overtures, and one morning, he received an ugly reward. Rapid as lightning, the cassowary hit straight from the hip and knee joints, and the elephant ran squealing to Grandfather.

For several days he avoided the cassowary, and we thought he had learnt his lesson. He crossed and recrossed the compound and the garden, swinging his trunk, thinking furiously. Then, a week later, he appeared on the veranda at breakfast time in his usual cheery, childlike fashion, sidling up to the cassowary as if nothing had happened.

We were struck with amazement at this and so, it seemed, was the bird. Had the painful lesson already been forgotten, and by a member of the elephant tribe noted for its ability to never forget? Another dose of the same medicine would serve the booby right.

The cassowary once more began to draw up its fighting leg with sinister determination. It was nearing the true position for the master kick, kung fu style, when all of a sudden the baby elephant seized with his trunk the cassowary's other leg and pulled it down. There was a clumsy flapping of wings, a tremendous swelling of the bird's wattle, and an undignified getting up, as if it were a floored boxer doing his best to beat the count of ten. The bird then marched off with an attempt to look stately and unconcerned, while we at the breakfast table were convulsed with laughter.

After this, the cassowary bird gave the baby elephant as wide a berth as possible. But they were not forced to coexist for very long. The baby elephant, getting bulky and cumbersome, was sold and now lives in a zoo where he is a favourite with young visitors who love to take rides on his back.

As for the cassowary, he continued to grace our veranda for many years, gaped at but not made much of, while entering on a rather friendless old age.

TIGERS FOREVER

~

May there always be tigers
In the jungles and tall grass.
May the tiger's roar be heard,
May his thunder
Be known in the land.
At the forest pool, by moonlight,
May he drink and raise his head,
Scenting the night wind.
May he crouch low in the grass
When the herdsmen pass,
And slumber in dark caverns
When the sun is high.
May there always be tigers.
But not so many, that one of them
Might be tempted to come into my room
In search of a meal!

THE TIGER IN THE TUNNEL

~

Tembu, the boy, opened his eyes in the dark and wondered if his father was ready to leave the hut on his nightly errand. There was no moon that night, and the deathly stillness of the surrounding jungle was broken only occasionally by the shrill cry of a cicada. Sometimes from far off came the hollow hammering of a woodpecker, carried along on the faint breeze. Or the grunt of a wild boar could be heard as he dug up a favourite root. But these sounds were rare, and the silence of the forest always returned to swallow them up.

Baldeo, the watchman, was awake. He stretched himself, slowly unwinding the heavy shawl that covered him like a shroud. It was close on midnight and the chilly air made him shiver. The station, a small shack backed by heavy jungle, was a station only in name; for trains only stopped there, if at all, for a few seconds before entering the deep cutting that led to the tunnel. Most trains merely slowed down before taking the sharp curve before the cutting.

Baldeo was responsible for signalling whether or not the tunnel was clear of obstruction, and his hand-worked signal stood before the entrance. At night, it was his duty to see that the lamp was burning, and that the overland mail passed through safely.

'Shall I come too, Father?' asked Tembu sleepily, still lying huddled in a corner of the hut.

'No, it is cold tonight. Do not get up.'

Tembu, who was twelve, did not always sleep with his father at the station, for he also had to help in the home, where his mother and small sister were usually alone. They lived in a small tribal village on the outskirts of the forest, about three miles from the station. Their small rice fields did not provide them with more than a bare living, and Baldeo considered himself lucky to have got the job of khalasi at this small wayside signal-stop.

Still drowsy, Baldeo groped for his lamp in the darkness, then fumbled about in search of matches. When he had produced a light, he left the hut, closed the door behind him, and set off along the permanent way. Tembu had fallen asleep again.

Baldeo wondered whether the lamp on the signal post was still alight. Gathering his shawl closer about him, he stumbled on, sometimes along the rails, sometimes along the ballast. He longed to get back to his warm corner in the hut.

The eeriness of the place was increased by the neighbouring hills, which overhung the main line threateningly. On entering the cutting, with its sheer rock walls towering high above the rails, Baldeo could not help thinking about the wild animals he might encounter. He had heard many tales of the famous tunnel tiger, a man-eater who was supposed to frequent this spot; but he hardly believed these stories for, since his arrival at this place a month ago, he had not seen or even heard a tiger.

There had, of course, been panthers, and only a few days previously the villagers had killed one with their spears and axes. Baldeo had occasionally heard the sawing of a panther calling to its mate, but they had not come near the tunnel or shed.

Baldeo walked confidently for, being a tribal himself, he was used to the jungle and its ways. Like his forefathers, he carried a small axe, fragile to look at, but deadly when in use. With it, in three or four swift strokes, he could cut down a tree as neatly as if it had been sawn; and he prided himself on his skill in wielding it against wild animals. He had killed a young boar with it once, and the family had feasted on the flesh for three days. The axe-head of pure steel, thin but ringing true like a bell, had been made by his father over a charcoal fire. This axe was a part of himself, and wherever he went, be it to the local market seven miles away, or to a tribal dance, the axe was always in his hand. Occasionally an official who had come to the station had offered him good money for the weapon; but Baldeo had no intention of parting with it.

The cutting curved sharply, and in the darkness, the black entrance to the tunnel loomed up menacingly. The signal light was out. Baldeo set to work to haul the lamp down by its chain. If the oil had finished, he would have to return to the hut for more. The mail train was due in five minutes.

Once more he fumbled for his matches. Then suddenly he stood still and listened. The frightened cry of a barking deer, followed by a crashing sound in the undergrowth, made Baldeo hurry. There was still a little oil in the lamp, and after an instant's hesitation he lit the lamp again and hoisted it back into position. Having done this, he walked quickly down the tunnel, swinging his own lamp, so that the shadows leapt up and down the soot-stained walls, and having made sure that the line was clear, he returned to the entrance and sat down to wait for the mail train.

The train was late. Sitting huddled up, almost dozing, he soon forgot his surroundings and began to nod off.

Back in the hut, the trembling of the ground told of the approach of the train, and a low, distant rumble woke the boy, who sat up, rubbing the sleep from his eyes.

'Father, it's time to light the lamp,' he mumbled, and then, realizing that his father had been gone some time, he lay down again; but he was wide awake now, waiting for the train to pass, waiting for his father's returning footsteps.

A low grunt resounded from the top of the cutting. In a second Baldeo was awake, all his senses alert. Only a tiger could emit such a sound.

There was no shelter for Baldeo, but he grasped his axe firmly and tensed his body, trying to make out the direction from which the animal was approaching. For some time there was only silence, even the usual jungle noises seemed to have ceased altogether. Then a thump and the rattle of small stones announced that the tiger had sprung into the cutting.

Baldeo, listening as he had never listened before, wondered if it was making for the tunnel or the opposite direction—the direction of the hut, in which Tembu would be lying unprotected. He did not have to wonder for long. Before a minute had passed, he made out the huge body of the tiger trotting steadily towards him. Its eyes shone a brilliant green in the light from the signal lamp. Flight was useless, for in the dark, the tiger would be more sure-footed than Baldeo and would soon be upon him from behind. Baldeo stood with his back to the signal post, motionless, staring at the great brute moving rapidly towards him. The tiger, used to the ways of men, for it had been preying on them for years, came on fearlessly, and with a quick run and a snarl struck out with its right paw, expecting to bowl over this puny man who dared stand in the way.

Baldeo, however, was ready. With a marvellously agile leap he avoided the paw and brought his axe down on the animal's shoulder. The tiger gave a roar and attempted to close in. Again Baldeo drove his axe with true aim; but, to his horror, the beast swerved, and the axe caught the tiger on the shoulder, almost severing the leg. To make matters worse, the axe remained stuck in the bone, and Baldeo was left without a weapon.

The tiger, roaring with pain, now sprang upon Baldeo, bringing him down and then tearing at his broken body. It was all over in a few minutes. Baldeo was conscious only of a searing pain down his back, and then there was blackness and the night closed in on him forever.

The tiger drew off and sat down licking his wounded leg,

roaring every now and then with agony. He did not notice the faint rumble that shook the earth, followed by the distant puffing of an engine steadily climbing. The overland mail was approaching. Through the trees beyond the cutting, as the train advanced, the glow of the furnace could be seen; and showers of sparks fell like Diwali lights over the forest.

As the train entered the cutting, the engine whistled once, loud and piercingly. The tiger raised his head, then slowly got to his feet. He found himself trapped like the man. Flight along the cutting was impossible. He entered the tunnel, running as fast as his wounded leg would carry him. And then, with a roar and a shower of sparks, the train entered the yawning tunnel. The noise in the confined space was deafening; but, when the train came out into the open, on the other side, silence returned once more to the forest and the tunnel.

At the next station, the driver slowed down and stopped his train to water the engine. He got down to stretch his legs and decided to examine the head-lamps. He received the surprise of his life; for, just above the cowcatcher lay the major portion of the tiger, cut in half by the engine.

There was considerable excitement and conjecture at the station, but back at the cutting there was no sound except for the sobs of the boy as he sat beside the body of his father. He sat there a long time, unafraid of the darkness, guarding the body from jackals and hyenas, until the first faint light of dawn brought with it the arrival of the relief watchman.

Tembu and his sister and mother were plunged in grief for two whole days; but life had to go on, and a living had to be made, and all the responsibility now fell on Tembu.

Three nights later, he was at the cutting, lighting the signal lamp for the overland mail.

He sat down in the darkness to wait for the train, and sang softly to himself. There was nothing to be afraid of—his father had killed the tiger, the forest gods were pleased; and besides, he had the axe with him, his father's axe, and he knew how to use it.

THE TREES

~

At seven, when dusk slips over the mountains,
The trees start whispering among themselves.
They have been standing still all day,
But now they stretch their limbs in the dark,
Shifting a little, flexing their fingers,
Remembering the time when
They, too, walked the earth with men.
They know me well, these trees:
Oak and walnut, spruce and pine,
They know my face in the window,
They know me for a dreamer of dreams,
A world-loser, one of them.
They watch me while I watch them grow.
I listen to their whisperings,
Their own mysterious diction;
And bow my head before their arms
And ask for benediction.

EXCITING ENCOUNTERS

~

Mehmoud, our cook, was making lamb chops. I liked lamb chops. Mehmoud knew I liked them, and he had an extra chop ready for me, just in case I felt like a pre-lunch snack.

'What was Jim Corbett's favourite dish?' I asked, while dealing with the succulent chop, for Mehmoud had once been the famous shikari's cook.

'Oh, he liked roast duck. Used to shoot them as they flew up from the jheel.'

'What's a jheel, Mehmoud?'

'A shallow sort of lake. In places you could walk about in the water. Different types of birds would come there in the winter—ducks and geese and all kinds of baglas—herons, you call them. The baglas are not good to eat, but the ducks make a fine roast. So we camped beside the jheel and lived on roast duck for a week until everyone was sick of it.'

'Did you go swimming in the jheel?'

'No, it was full of muggers—those long-nosed crocodiles—they'll snap you up if you come within their range! Nasty creatures, those muggermuch. One of them nearly got me.'

'How did that happen, Mehmoud-bhai?'

'Oh, baba, just the memory of it makes me shudder! I'd given everyone their dinner and retired to my tent. It was a hot night and we couldn't sleep. Swarms of mosquitoes rose from the jheel, invaded the tent, and attacked me on the face and arms and feet. I dragged my camp cot outside the tent, hoping the breeze would keep the mosquitoes away. After some time they moved on, and I fell asleep, wrapped up in my bedsheet. Towards dawn, I felt my cot quivering, shaking. Was it an earthquake? But no one else was awake. And then the cot started moving! I sat up, looked about me. The cot was moving steadily forward in the direction of the water. And beneath it, holding us up, was a beastly crocodile!

'It gave me the fright of my life, baba. A muggermuch beneath my bed, and I upon it! I cried out for help. Carpet-sahib woke up, rushed out of his tent, his gun in his hands. But it was still dark, and all he could see was my moving rapidly towards the jheel.

'Just before we struck the water, I leapt from the cot, and ran up the bank, calling for help. Carpet-sahib saw me then. He ran down the slope, firing at the moving cot. I don't know if he hit the horrible creature, but there was a big splash, and it disappeared into the jheel.'

'And did you recover the cot?'

'No, it floated away and then sank. We did not go after it.'

'And what did Corbett say afterwards?'

'He said I had shown great presence of mind. He said he'd never seen anyone make such a leap for safety!'

'You were a hero, Mehmoud!'

'Thank you, baba. There's time for another lamb chop, if you're hungry.'

'I'm hungry,' I said. 'There's still an hour left to lunchtime. But tell me more about your time with Jim Corbett. Did he like your cooking?'

'Oh, *he* liked it well enough, but his sister was very fussy.'

'He had his sister with him?'

'That's right. He never married, so his sister looked after the household and the shopping and everything connected to the kitchen—except when we were in camp. Then I had a free hand. Carpet-sahib wasn't too fussy about his food, especially when he was out hunting. A sandwich or paratha would keep him going. But if he had guests, he felt he had to give them the best, and then it was hard work for me.

'For instance, there was the Raja of Janakpur, a big fat man who was very fond of eating—between meals, during meals and after meals. I don't know why he bothered to come on these shikar trips when he could have stayed at home in his palace and feasted day and night. But he needed trophies to hang on the walls of his palace. You were not considered a great king unless your walls were decorated with the stuffed heads of tigers, lions, antelopes, bears—anything that looked dangerous. The Raja could eat and drink all day, but he couldn't go home without a trophy. So he would be hoisted on to an elephant, and sit there in state, firing away at anything that moved in the jungle. He seldom shot anything, but Carpet-sahib would help him out by bringing down a stag or a leopard, and congratulating the Raja on his skill and accuracy.

'They weren't all like that, but some of the rajas were stupid or even mad. And the Angrej-sahibs—the English—were no better. They, too, had to prove their manliness by shooting a tiger or a leopard. Carpet-sahib was always in demand, because he lived at the edge of the jungle and knew where to look for different animals.

'The Raja of Janakpur was safe on an elephant, but one day he made the mistake of walking into the jungle on foot. He hadn't gone far when he met a wild boar running at him. A wild boar may not look very dangerous, but it has deadly tusks and is quick to use them. Before the Raja could raise the gun to his shoulder, the pig charged at him. The Raja dropped his gun, turned and ran for his life. But he couldn't run very fast or very far. He tripped and fell, and the boar was almost upon him when I happened along, looking for twigs to make a fire. Luckily, I had a small axe in my hand. I struck the boar over the head. It turned and rammed one of its tusks into my thigh. I struck at it again and again, till it fell dead at my feet. The Raja was nowhere in sight.

'As soon as he got into camp, he sent for his servants and made a hurried departure. Didn't even thank me for saving his life.'

'Were you hurt badly, Mehmoud?'

'I was out of action for a few days. The wound took time to heal. My new masalchi did all the cooking, and the food was so bad that most of the guests left in a hurry. I still have the scar. See, baba!'

Mehmoud drew up his pyjamas and showed me a deep scar on his right thigh.

'You were a hero, Mehmoud,' I said. 'You deserved a reward.'

'My reward is here, baba, preparing these lamb chops for you. Come on, have another. Your parents won't notice if they run short at lunch.'

ANGRY RIVER

~

In the middle of the big river, the river that began in the mountains and ended in the sea, was a small island. The river swept round the island, sometimes clawing at its banks, but never going right over it. It was over twenty years since the river had flooded the island, and at that time no one had lived there. But for the last ten years a small hut had stood there, a mud-walled hut with a sloping thatched roof. The hut had been built into a huge rock, so only three of the walls were mud, and the fourth was rock.

Goats grazed on the short grass which grew on the island, and on the prickly leaves of thorn bushes. A few hens followed them about. There was a melon patch and a vegetable patch.

In the middle of the island stood a peepul tree. It was the only tree there.

Even during the Great Flood, when the island had been under water, the tree had stood firm.

It was an old tree. A seed had been carried to the island by a strong wind some fifty years back, had found shelter between two rocks, had taken root there, and had sprung up to give shade and shelter to a small family; and Indians love peepul trees, especially during the hot summer months when the heart-shaped leaves catch the least breath of air and flutter eagerly, fanning those who sit beneath.

A sacred tree, the peepul: the abode of spirits, good and bad.

'Don't yawn when you are sitting beneath the tree,' Grandmother used to warn Sita. 'And if you must yawn, always snap your fingers in front of your mouth. If you forget to do that, a spirit might jump down your throat!'

'And then what will happen?' asked Sita.

'It will probably ruin your digestion,' said Grandfather, who wasn't much of a believer in spirits.

The peepul had a beautiful leaf, and Grandmother likened it to the body of the mighty god Krishna—broad at the shoulders, then tapering down to a very slim waist.

It was an old tree, and an old man sat beneath it.

He was mending a fishing net. He had fished in the river for ten years, and he was a good fisherman. He knew where to find the slim silver chilwa fish and the big beautiful mahseer and the long-moustached singhara; he knew where the river was deep and where it was shallow; he knew which baits to use—which fish liked worms and which liked gram. He had taught his son to fish, but his son had gone to work in a factory in a city, nearly a hundred miles away. He had no grandson; but he had a granddaughter, Sita, and she could do all the things a boy could do, and sometimes she could do them better. She had lost her mother when she was very small. Grandmother had taught her all the things a girl should know, and she could do these as well as most girls. But neither of her grandparents could read or write, and as a result Sita couldn't read or write either.

There was a school in one of the villages across the river, but Sita had never seen it. There was too much to do on the island.

While Grandfather mended his net, Sita was inside the hut, pressing her Grandmother's forehead, which was hot with fever. Grandmother had been ill for three days and could not eat. She had been ill before, but she had never been so bad. Grandfather had brought her some sweet oranges from the market in the nearest town, and she could suck the juice from the oranges, but she couldn't eat anything else.

She was younger than Grandfather, but because she was sick, she looked much older. She had never been very strong.

When Sita noticed that Grandmother had fallen asleep, she tiptoed out of the room on her bare feet and stood outside.

The sky was dark with monsoon clouds. It had rained all night, and in a few hours it would rain again. The monsoon rains had come early, at the end of June. Now it was the middle of July, and already the river was swollen. Its rushing sound seemed nearer and more menacing than usual.

Sita went to Grandfather and sat down beside him beneath the peepul tree.

'When you are hungry, tell me,' she said, 'and I will make the bread.'

'Is your grandmother asleep?'

'She sleeps. But she will wake soon, for she has a deep pain.'

The old man stared out across the river, at the dark green of the forest, at the grey sky, and said, 'Tomorrow, if she is not better, I will take her to the hospital at Shahganj. There they will know how to make her well. You may be on your own for a few days—but you have been on your own before...'

Sita nodded gravely; she had been alone before, even during the rainy season. Now she wanted Grandmother to get well, and she knew that only Grandfather had the skill to take the small dugout boat across the river when the current was so strong. Someone would have to stay behind to look after their few possessions.

Sita was not afraid of being alone, but she did not like the look of the river. That morning, when she had gone down to fetch water, she had noticed that the level had risen. Those rocks which were normally spattered with the droppings of snipe and curlew and other waterbirds had suddenly disappeared.

They disappeared every year—but not so soon, surely?

'Grandfather, if the river rises, what will I do?'

'You will keep to the high ground.'

'And if the water reaches the high ground?'

'Then take the hens into the hut, and stay there.'

'And if the water comes into the hut?'

'Then climb the peepul tree. It is a strong tree. It will not fall. And the water cannot rise higher than the tree!'

'And the goats, Grandfather?'

'I will be taking them with me, Sita. I may have to sell them to pay for good food and medicines for your grandmother. As for the hens, if it becomes necessary, put them on the roof. But do not worry too much'—and he patted Sita's head—'the water will not rise as high. I will be back soon, remember that.'

'And won't Grandmother come back?'

'Yes, of course, but they may keep her in the hospital for some time.'

~

Towards evening, it began to rain again—big pellets of rain, scarring the surface of the river. But it was warm rain, and Sita could move about in it. She was not afraid of getting wet, she rather liked it. In the previous month, when the first monsoon shower had arrived, washing the dusty leaves of the tree and bringing up the good smell of the earth, she had exulted in it, had run about shouting for joy. She was used to it now, and indeed a little tired of the rain, but she did not mind getting wet. It was steamy indoors, and her thin dress would soon dry in the heat from the kitchen fire.

She walked about barefooted, barelegged. She was very sure on her feet; her toes had grown accustomed to gripping all kinds of rocks, slippery or sharp. And though thin, she was surprisingly strong.

Black hair, streaming across her face. Black eyes. Slim brown arms. A scar on her thigh—when she was small, visiting her mother's village, a hyena had entered the house where she was sleeping, fastened on to her leg and tried to drag her away, but her screams had roused the villagers and the hyena had run off.

She moved about in the pouring rain, chasing the hens into a shelter behind the hut. A harmless brown snake, flooded out of its hole, was moving across the open ground. Sita picked up a stick, scooped the snake up, and dropped it between a cluster of rocks. She had no quarrel with snakes. They kept down the rats and the frogs. She wondered how the rats had first come to the island—probably in someone's boat, or in a sack of grain. Now it was a job to keep their numbers down.

When Sita finally went indoors, she was hungry. She ate some dried peas and warmed up some goat's milk.

Grandmother woke once and asked for water, and Grandfather held the brass tumbler to her lips.

~

It rained all night.

The roof was leaking, and a small puddle formed on the floor. They kept the kerosene lamp alight. They did not need the light, but somehow it made them feel safer.

The sound of the river had always been with them, although they were seldom aware of it; but that night they noticed a change in its sound. There was something like a moan, like a wind in the tops of tall trees, and a swift hiss as the water swept round the rocks and carried away pebbles. And sometimes there was a rumble, as loose earth fell into the water.

Sita could not sleep.

She had a rag doll, made with Grandmother's help out of bits of old clothing. She kept it by her side every night.

The doll was someone to talk to, when the nights were long and sleep elusive. Her grandparents were often ready to talk—and Grandmother, when she was well, was a good storyteller—but sometimes Sita wanted to have secrets, and though there were no special secrets in her life, she made up a few, because it was fun to have them. And if you have secrets, you must have a friend to share them with, a companion of one's own age. Since there were no other children on the island, Sita shared her secrets with the rag doll whose name was Mumta.

Grandfather and Grandmother were asleep, though the sound of Grandmother's laboured breathing was almost as persistent as the sound of the river.

'Mumta,' whispered Sita in the dark, starting one of her private conversations. 'Do you think Grandmother will get well again?'

Mumta always answered Sita's questions, even though the answers could only be heard by Sita.

'She is very old,' said Mumta.

'Do you think the river will reach the hut?' asked Sita.

'If it keeps raining like this, and the river keeps rising, it will reach the hut.'

'I am a little afraid of the river, Mumta. Aren't you afraid?'

'Don't be afraid. The river has always been good to us.'

'What will we do if it comes into the hut?'

'We will climb on to the roof.'

'And if it reaches the roof?'

'We will climb the peepul tree. The river has never gone higher than the peepul tree.'

As soon as the first light showed through the little skylight,

Sita got up and went outside. It wasn't raining hard, it was drizzling, but it was the sort of drizzle that could continue for days, and it probably meant that heavy rain was falling in the hills where the river originated.

Sita went down to the water's edge. She couldn't find her favourite rock, the one on which she often sat dangling her feet in the water, watching the little chilwa fish swim by. It was still there, no doubt, but the river had gone over it.

She stood on the sand, and she could feel the water oozing and bubbling beneath her feet.

The river was no longer green and blue and flecked with white, but a muddy colour.

She went back to the hut. Grandfather was up now. He was getting his boat ready.

Sita milked the goat. Perhaps it was the last time she would milk it.

~

The sun was just coming up when Grandfather pushed off in the boat. Grandmother lay in the prow. She was staring hard at Sita, trying to speak, but the words would not come. She raised her hand in a blessing.

Sita bent and touched her grandmother's feet, and then Grandfather pushed off. The little boat—with its two old people and three goats—riding swiftly on the river, moved slowly, very slowly, towards the opposite bank. The current was so swift now that Sita realized the boat would be carried about half a mile downstream before Grandfather could get it to dry land.

It bobbed about on the water, getting smaller and smaller, until it was just a speck on the broad river.

And suddenly Sita was alone.

There was a wind, whipping the raindrops against her face; and there was the water, rushing past the island; and there was the distant shore, blurred by rain; and there was the small hut; and there was the tree.

Sita got busy. The hens had to be fed. They weren't bothered about anything except food. Sita threw them handfuls of coarse grain and potato peelings and peanut shells.

Then she took the broom and swept out the hut, lit the charcoal burner, warmed some milk and thought, 'Tomorrow there will be no milk...' She began peeling onions. Soon her eyes started smarting and, pausing for a few moments and glancing round the quiet room, she became aware again that she was alone. Grandfather's hookah pipe stood by itself in one corner. It was a beautiful old hookah, which had belonged to Sita's great-grandfather. The bowl was made out of a coconut encased in silver. The long winding stem was at least four feet in length. It was their most valuable possession. Grandmother's sturdy sheesham-wood walking stick stood in another corner.

Sita looked around for Mumta, found the doll beneath the cot, and placed her within sight and hearing.

Thunder rolled down from the hills. BOOM—BOOM—BOOM...

'The gods of the mountains are angry,' said Sita. 'Do you think they are angry with me?'

'Why should they be angry with you?' asked Mumta.

'They don't have to have a reason for being angry. They are

angry with everything, and we are in the middle of everything. We are so small—do you think they know we are here?'

'Who knows what the gods think?'

'But I made you,' said Sita, 'and I know you are here.'

'And will you save me if the river rises?'

'Yes, of course. I won't go anywhere without you, Mumta.'

Sita couldn't stay indoors for long. She went out, taking Mumta with her, and stared out across the river, to the safe land on the other side. But was it safe there? The river looked much wider now. Yes, it had crept over its banks and spread far across the flat plain. Far away, people were driving their cattle through waterlogged, flooded fields, carrying their belongings in bundles on their heads or shoulders, leaving their homes, making for the high land. It wasn't safe anywhere.

She wondered what had happened to Grandfather and Grandmother. If they had reached the shore safely, Grandfather would have to engage a bullock cart, or a pony-drawn carriage to get Grandmother to the district town, five or six miles away, where there was a market, a court, a jail, a cinema and a hospital.

She wondered if she would ever see Grandmother again. She had done her best to look after the old lady, remembering the times when Grandmother had looked after her, had gently touched her fevered brow and had told her stories—stories about the gods: about the young Krishna, friend of birds and animals, so full of mischief, always causing confusion among the other gods; and Indra, who made thunder and lightning; and Vishnu, the preserver of all good things, whose steed was a great white bird; and Ganesh, with the elephant's head; and Hanuman, the monkey-god, who helped the young Prince Rama in his war with the King of Ceylon. Would Grandmother return to tell her more about them, or would she have to find out for herself?

The island looked much smaller now. In parts, the mud banks had dissolved quickly, sinking into the river. But in the middle of the island there was rocky ground, and the rocks would never crumble, they could only be submerged. In a space in the middle of the rocks grew the tree.

Sita climbed the tree to get a better view. She had climbed the tree many times and it took her only a few seconds to reach the higher branches. She put her hand to her eyes to shield them from the rain, and gazed upstream.

There was water everywhere. The world had become one vast river. Even the trees on the forested side of the river looked as though they had grown from the water, like mangroves. The sky was banked with massive, moisture-laden clouds. Thunder rolled down from the hills and the river seemed to take it up with a hollow booming sound.

Something was floating down with the current, something big and bloated. It was closer now, and Sita could make out the bulky object—a drowned buffalo, being carried rapidly downstream.

So the water had already inundated the villages further upstream. Or perhaps the buffalo had been grazing too close to the rising river.

Sita's worst fears were confirmed when, a little later, she saw planks of wood, small trees and bushes, and then a wooden bedstead, floating past the island.

How long would it take for the river to reach her own small hut?

As she climbed down from the tree, it began to rain more heavily. She ran indoors, shooing the hens before her. They flew into the hut and huddled under Grandmother's cot. Sita thought it would be best to keep them together now. And having them with her took away some of the loneliness.

There were three hens and a cock bird. The river did not bother them. They were interested only in food, and Sita kept them happy by throwing them a handful of onion skins.

She would have liked to close the door and shut out the swish of the rain and the boom of the river, but then she would have no way of knowing how fast the water rose.

She took Mumta in her arms, and began praying for the rain to stop and the river to fall. She prayed to the god Indra, and, just in case he was busy elsewhere, she prayed to other gods too. She prayed for the safety of her grandparents and for her own safety. She put herself last but only with great difficulty.

She would have to make herself a meal. So she chopped up some onions, fried them, then added turmeric and red chilli powder and stirred until she had everything sizzling; then she added a tumbler of water, some salt, and a cup of one of the cheaper lentils. She covered the pot and allowed the mixture to simmer.

Doing this took Sita about ten minutes. It would take at least half an hour for the dish to be ready.

When she looked outside, she saw pools of water amongst the rocks and near the tree. She couldn't tell if it was rain water or overflow from the river.

She had an idea.

A big tin trunk stood in a corner of the room. It had belonged to Sita's mother. There was nothing in it except a cotton-filled quilt, for use during the cold weather. She would stuff the trunk with everything useful or valuable, and weigh it down so that it wouldn't be carried away, just in case the river came over the island.

Grandfather's hookah went into the trunk. Grandmother's walking stick went in too. So did a number of small tins containing the spices used in cooking—nutmeg, caraway seed, cinnamon, coriander and pepper—a bigger tin of flour and a tin of raw sugar. Even if Sita had to spend several hours in the tree, there would be something to eat when she came down again.

A clean white cotton shirt of Grandfather's, and Grandmother's only spare sari also went into the trunk. Never mind if they got stained with yellow curry powder! Never mind if they got to smell of salted fish, some of that went in too.

Sita was so busy packing the trunk that she paid no attention to the lick of cold water at her heels. She locked the trunk, placed the key high on the rock wall, and turned to give her attention to the lentils. It was only then that she discovered that she was walking about on a watery floor.

She stood still, horrified by what she saw. The water was oozing over the threshold, pushing its way into the room.

Sita was filled with panic. She forgot about her meal and everything else. Darting out of the hut, she ran splashing through ankle-deep water towards the safety of the peepul tree. If the tree hadn't been there, such a well-known landmark, she might have floundered into deep water, into the river.

She climbed swiftly up the strong arms of the tree, made herself secure on a familiar branch, and thrust the wet hair away from her eyes.

~

She was glad she had hurried. The hut was now surrounded by water. Only the higher parts of the island could still be seen—a few rocks, the big rock on which the hut was built, a hillock on which some thorny bilberry bushes grew.

The hens hadn't bothered to leave the hut. They were probably perched on the cot now.

Would the river rise still higher? Sita had never seen it like this before. It swirled around her, stretching in all directions.

More drowned cattle came floating down. The most unusual things went by on the water—an aluminium kettle, a cane chair, a tin of tooth powder, an empty cigarette packet, a wooden slipper, a plastic doll...

A doll!

With a sinking feeling, Sita remembered Mumta.

Poor Mumta! She had been left behind in the hut. Sita, in her hurry, had forgotten her only companion.

Well, thought Sita, if I can be careless with someone I've made, how can I expect the gods to notice me, alone in the middle of the river?

The waters were higher now, the island fast disappearing.

Something came floating out of the hut.

It was an empty kerosene tin, with one of the hens perched

on top. The tin came bobbing along on the water, not far from the tree, and was then caught by the current and swept into the river. The hen still managed to keep its perch.

A little later, the water must have reached the cot because the remaining hens flew up to the rock ledge and sat huddled there in the small recess.

The water was rising rapidly now, and all that remained of the island was the big rock that supported the hut, the top of the hut itself and the peepul tree.

It was a tall tree with many branches and it seemed unlikely that the water could ever go right over it. But how long would Sita have to remain there? She climbed a little higher, and as she did so, a jet-black jungle crow settled in the upper branches, and Sita saw that there was a nest in them—a crow's nest, an untidy platform of twigs wedged in the fork of a branch.

In the nest were four blue-green, speckled eggs. The crow sat on them and cawed disconsolately. But though the crow was miserable, its presence brought some cheer to Sita. At least she was not alone. Better to have a crow for company than no one at all.

Other things came floating out of the hut—a large pumpkin; a red turban belonging to Grandfather, unwinding in the water like a long snake; and then—Mumta!

The doll, being filled with straw and wood-shavings, moved quite swiftly on the water and passed close to the peepul tree. Sita saw it and wanted to call out, to urge her friend to make for the tree, but she knew that Mumta could not swim—the doll could only float, travel with the river, and perhaps be washed ashore many miles downstream.

The tree shook in the wind and the rain. The crow cawed and flew up, circled the tree a few times and returned to the nest. Sita clung to her branch.

The tree trembled throughout its tall frame. To Sita it felt like an earthquake tremor; she felt the shudder of the tree in her own bones.

The river swirled all around her now. It was almost up to the roof of the hut. Soon the mud walls would crumble and vanish. Except for the big rock and some trees far, far away, there was only water to be seen.

For a moment or two, Sita glimpsed a boat with several people in it moving sluggishly away from the ruins of a flooded village, and she thought she saw someone pointing towards her, but the river swept them on and the boat was lost to view.

The river was very angry; it was like a wild beast, a dragon on the rampage, thundering down from the hills and sweeping across the plain, bringing with it dead animals, uprooted trees, household goods and huge fish choked to death by the swirling mud.

The tall old peepul tree groaned. Its long, winding roots clung tenaciously to the earth from which the tree had sprung many, many years ago. But the earth was softening, the stones were being washed away. The roots of the tree were rapidly losing their hold.

The crow must have known that something was wrong, because it kept flying up and circling the tree, reluctant to settle in it and reluctant to fly away. As long as the nest was there, the crow would remain, flapping about and cawing in alarm.

Sita's wet cotton dress clung to her thin body. The rain ran down from her long black hair. It poured from every leaf of the tree. The crow, too, was drenched and groggy.

The tree groaned and moved again. It had seen many monsoons. Once before, it had stood firm while the river had swirled around its massive trunk. But it had been young then.

Now, old in years and tired of standing still, the tree was ready to join the river.

With a flurry of its beautiful leaves, and a surge of mud from below, the tree left its place in the earth, tilting, moved slowly forward, turning a little from side to side, dragging its roots along the ground. To Sita, it seemed as though the river was rising to meet the sky. Then the tree moved into the main current of the river, and went a little faster, swinging Sita from side to side. Her feet were in the water but she clung tenaciously to her branch.

∼

The branches swayed, but Sita did not lose her grip. The water was very close now. Sita was frightened. She could not see the extent of the flood or the width of the river. She could only see the immediate danger—the water surrounding the tree.

The crow kept flying around the tree. The bird was in a terrible rage. The nest was still in the branches, but not for long... The tree lurched and twisted slightly to one side, and the nest fell into the water. Sita saw the eggs go one by one.

The crow swooped low over the water, but there was nothing it could do. In a few moments, the nest had disappeared.

The bird followed the tree for about fifty yards, as though

hoping that something still remained in the tree. Then, flapping its wings, it rose high into the air and flew across the river until it was out of sight.

Sita was alone once more. But there was no time to feel lonely. Everything was in motion—up and down and sideways and forwards. 'Any moment,' thought Sita, 'the tree will turn right over and I'll be in the water!'

She saw a turtle swimming past—a great river turtle, the kind that feeds on decaying flesh. Sita turned her face away. In the distance she saw a flooded village and people in flat-bottomed boats, but they were very far away.

Because of its great size, the tree did not move very swiftly on the river. Sometimes, when it passed into shallow water, it stopped, its roots catching in the rocks; but not for long—the river's momentum soon swept it on.

At one place, where there was a bend in the river, the tree struck a sandbank and was still.

Sita felt very tired. Her arms were aching and she was no longer upright. With the tree almost on its side, she had to cling tightly to her branch to avoid falling off. The grey weeping sky was like a great shifting dome.

She knew she could not remain much longer in that position. It might be better to try swimming to some distant rooftop or tree. Then she heard someone calling. Craning her neck to look upriver, she was able to make out a small boat coming directly towards her.

The boat approached the tree. There was a boy in the boat who held on to one of the branches to steady himself, giving his free hand to Sita.

She grasped it, and slipped into the boat beside him.

The boy placed his bare foot against the tree trunk and pushed away.

The little boat moved swiftly down the river. The big tree was left far behind. Sita would never see it again.

~

She lay stretched out in the boat, too frightened to talk. The boy looked at her, but he did not say anything, he did not even smile. He lay on his two small oars, stroking smoothly, rhythmically, trying to keep from going into the middle of the river. He wasn't strong enough to get the boat right out of the swift current, but he kept trying.

A small boat on a big river—a river that had no boundaries but which reached across the plains in all directions. The boat moved swiftly on the wild waters, and Sita's home was left far behind.

The boy wore only a loincloth. A sheathed knife was knotted into his waistband. He was a slim, wiry boy, with a hard flat belly; he had high cheekbones, strong white teeth. He was a little darker than Sita.

'You live on the island,' he said at last, resting on his oars and allowing the boat to drift a little, for he had reached a broader, more placid stretch of the river. 'I have seen you sometimes. But where are the others?'

'My grandmother was sick,' said Sita. 'So Grandfather took her to the hospital in Shahganj.'

'When did they leave?'

'Early this morning.'

Only that morning—and yet it seemed to Sita as though it had been many mornings ago.

'Where have you come from?' she asked. She had never seen the boy before.

'I come from...' he hesitated, '...near the foothills. I was in my boat, trying to get across the river with the news that one of the villages was badly flooded, but the current was too strong. I was swept down past your island. We cannot fight the river, we must go wherever it takes us.'

'You must be tired. Give me the oars.'

'No. There is not much to do now, except keep the boat steady.'

He brought in one oar, and with his free hand he felt under the seat where there was a small basket. He produced two mangoes, and gave one to Sita.

They bit deep into the ripe fleshy mangoes, using their teeth to tear the skin away. The sweet juice trickled down their chins. The flavour of the fruit was heavenly—truly this was the nectar of the gods! Sita hadn't tasted a mango for over a year. For a few moments she forgot about the flood—all that mattered was the mango!

The boat drifted, but not so swiftly now, for as they went further away across the plains, the river lost much of its tremendous force.

'My name is Krishan,' said the boy. 'My father has many cows and buffaloes, but several have been lost in the flood.'

'I suppose you go to school,' said Sita.

'Yes, I am supposed to go to school. There is one not far from our village. Do you have to go to school?'

'No—there is too much work at home.'

It was no use wishing she was at home—home wouldn't be there any more—but she wished, at that moment, that she had another mango.

Towards evening, the river changed colour. The sun, low in the sky, emerged from behind the clouds, and the river changed slowly from grey to gold, from gold to a deep orange, and then, as the sun went down, all these colours were drowned in the river, and the river took on the colour of the night.

The moon was almost at the full and Sita could see across the river, to where the trees grew on its banks.

'I will try to reach the trees,' said the boy Krishan. 'We do not want to spend the night on the water, do we?'

And so he pulled for the trees. After ten minutes of strenuous rowing, he reached a turn in the river and was able to escape the pull of the main current.

Soon they were in a forest, rowing between tall evergreens.

~

They moved slowly now, paddling between the trees, and the moon lit their way, making a crooked silver path over the water.

'We will tie the boat to one of these trees,' said Krishan. 'Then we can rest. Tomorrow we will have to find our way out of the forest.'

He produced a length of rope from the bottom of the boat, tied one end to the boat's stern and threw the other end over a stout branch which hung only a few feet above the water. The boat came to rest against the trunk of the tree.

It was a tall, sturdy toon tree—the Indian mahogany—

and it was quite safe, for there was no rush of water here; besides, the trees grew close together, making the earth firm and unyielding.

But the denizens of the forest were on the move. The animals had been flooded out of their holes, caves and lairs, and were looking for shelter and dry ground.

Sita and Krishan had barely finished tying the boat to the tree when they saw a huge python gliding over the water towards them. Sita was afraid that it might try to get into the boat; but it went past them, its head above water, its great awesome length trailing behind, until it was lost in the shadows.

Krishan had more mangoes in the basket, and he and Sita sucked hungrily on them while they sat in the boat.

A big sambur stag came thrashing through the water. He did not have to swim; he was so tall that his head and shoulders remained well above the water. His antlers were big and beautiful.

'There will be other animals,' said Sita. 'Should we climb into the tree?'

'We are quite safe in the boat,' said Krishan. 'The animals are interested only in reaching dry land. They will not even hunt each other. Tonight, the deer are safe from the panther and the tiger. So lie down and sleep, and I will keep watch.'

Sita stretched herself out in the boat and closed her eyes, and the sound of the water lapping against the sides of the boat soon lulled her to sleep. She woke once, when a strange bird called overhead. She raised herself on one elbow, but Krishan was awake, sitting in the prow, and he smiled reassuringly at her. He looked blue in the moonlight, the colour of the young god Krishna, and for a few moments Sita was confused and wondered if the boy was indeed Krishna; but when she thought about it, she decided that it wasn't possible. He was just a village boy and she had seen hundreds like him—well, not exactly like him; he was different, in a way she couldn't explain to herself...

And when she slept again, she dreamt that the boy and Krishna were one, and that she was sitting beside him on a great white bird which flew over mountains, over the snow peaks of the Himalayas, into the cloud-land of the gods. There was a great rumbling sound, as though the gods were angry about the whole thing, and she woke up to this terrible sound and looked about her, and there in the moonlit glade, up to his belly in water, stood a young elephant, his trunk raised as he trumpeted his predicament to the forest—for he was a young elephant, and he was lost, and he was looking for his mother.

He trumpeted again, and then lowered his head and listened. And presently, from far away, came the shrill trumpeting of another elephant. It must have been the young one's mother, because he gave several excited trumpet calls, and then went stamping and churning through the flood water towards a gap in the trees. The boat rocked in the waves made by his passing.

'It's all right now,' said Krishan. 'You can go to sleep again.'

'I don't think I will sleep now,' said Sita.

'Then I will play my flute for you,' said the boy, 'and the time will pass more quickly.'

From the bottom of the boat he took a flute, and putting it to his lips, he began to play. The sweetest music that Sita had ever heard came pouring from the little flute, and it seemed to fill the forest with its beautiful sound. And the music carried her away again, into the land of dreams, and they were riding on the bird once more, Sita and the blue god, and they were passing through clouds and mist, until suddenly the sun shot out through the clouds. And at the same moment, Sita opened her eyes and saw the sun streaming through the branches of the toon tree, its bright green leaves making a dark pattern against the blinding blue of the sky.

Sita sat up with a start, rocking the boat. There were hardly any clouds left. The trees were drenched with sunshine.

The boy Krishan was fast asleep in the bottom of the boat. His flute lay in the palm of his half-open hand. The sun came slanting across his bare brown legs. A leaf had fallen on his upturned face, but it had not woken him, it lay on his cheek as though it had grown there.

Sita did not move again. She did not want to wake the boy. It didn't look as though the water had gone down, but it hadn't risen, and that meant the flood had spent itself.

The warmth of the sun, as it crept up Krishan's body, woke him at last. He yawned, stretched his limbs, and sat up beside Sita.

'I'm hungry,' he said with a smile.

'So am I,' said Sita.

'The last mangoes,' he said, and emptied the basket of its last two mangoes.

After they had finished the fruit, they sucked the big seeds until these were quite dry. The discarded seeds floated well on the water. Sita had always preferred them to paper boats.

'We had better move on,' said Krishan.

He rowed the boat through the trees, and then for about an hour they were passing through the flooded forest, under the dripping branches of rain-washed trees. Sometimes they had to use the oars to push away vines and creepers. Sometimes drowned bushes hampered them. But they were out of the forest before noon.

Now the water was not very deep and they were gliding over flooded fields. In the distance they saw a village. It was on high ground. In the old days, people had built their villages on hilltops, which gave them better defence against bandits and invading armies. This was an old village, and though its inhabitants had long ago exchanged their swords for pruning forks, the hill on which it stood now protected it from the flood.

The people of the village—long-limbed, sturdy Jats—were generous, and gave the stranded children food and shelter. Sita was anxious to find her grandparents, and an old farmer who had business in Shahganj offered to take her there. She was hoping that Krishan would accompany her, but he said he would wait in the village, where he knew others would soon be arriving, his own people among them.

'You will be all right now,' said Krishan. 'Your grandfather will be anxious for you, so it is best that you go to him as soon as you can. And in two or three days, the water will go down and you will be able to return to the island.'

'Perhaps the island has gone forever,' said Sita.

As she climbed into the farmer's bullock cart, Krishan handed her his flute.

'Please keep it for me,' he said. 'I will come for it one day.' And when he saw her hesitate, he added, his eyes twinkling, 'It is a good flute!'

≈

It was slow going in the bullock cart. The road was awash, the wheels got stuck in the mud, and the farmer, his grown son and Sita had to keep getting down to heave and push in order to free the big wooden wheels. They were still in a foot or two of water. The bullocks were bespattered with mud, and Sita's legs were caked with it.

They were a day and a night in the bullock cart before they reached Shahganj; by that time, Sita, walking down the narrow bazaar of the busy market town, was hardly recognizable.

Grandfather did not recognize her. He was walking stiffly down the road, looking straight ahead of him, and would have walked right past the dusty, dishevelled girl if she had not charged straight at his thin, shaky legs and clasped him around the waist.

'Sita!' he cried, when he had recovered his wind and his balance. 'But how are you here? How did you get off the island? I was so worried—it has been very bad these last two days...'

'Is Grandmother all right?' asked Sita.

But even as she spoke, she knew that Grandmother was no longer with them. The dazed look in the old man's eyes told her as much. She wanted to cry, not for Grandmother, who could suffer no more, but for Grandfather, who looked so helpless and bewildered; she did not want him to be unhappy. She forced back her tears, took his gnarled and trembling hand, and led him down the crowded street. And she knew then that it would be on her shoulder that Grandfather would have to lean in the years to come.

They returned to the island after a few days, when the river was no longer in spate. There was more rain, but the worst was over. Grandfather still had two of the goats; it had not been necessary to sell more than one.

He could hardly believe his eyes when he saw that the tree had disappeared from the island—the tree that had seemed as permanent as the island, as much a part of his life as the river itself. He marvelled at Sita's escape. 'It was the tree that saved you,' he said.

'And the boy,' said Sita.

Yes, and the boy.

She thought about the boy, and wondered if she would ever see him again. But she did not think too much, because there was so much to do.

For three nights they slept under a crude shelter made out of jute bags. During the day she helped Grandfather rebuild the mud hut. Once again, they used the big rock as a support.

The trunk which Sita had packed so carefully had not been swept off the island, but the water had got into it, and the food and clothing had been spoilt. But Grandfather's hookah had been saved, and, in the evenings, after their work was done and they had eaten the light meal which Sita prepared, he would smoke with a little of his old contentment, and tell

Sita about other floods and storms which he had experienced as a boy.

Sita planted a mango seed in the same spot where the peepul tree had stood. It would be many years before it grew into a big tree, but Sita liked to imagine sitting in its branches one day, picking the mangoes straight from the tree, and feasting on them all day. Grandfather was more particular about making a vegetable garden and putting down peas, carrots, gram and mustard.

One day, when most of the hard work had been done and the new hut was almost ready, Sita took the flute which had been given to her by the boy, and walked down to the water's edge and tried to play it. But all she could produce were a few broken notes, and even the goats paid no attention to her music.

Sometimes Sita thought she saw a boat coming down the river and she would run to meet it; but usually there was no boat, or if there was, it belonged to a stranger or to another fisherman. And so she stopped looking out for boats. Sometimes she thought she heard the music of a flute, but it seemed very distant and she could never tell where the music came from.

Slowly, the rains came to an end. The flood waters had receded, and in the villages people were beginning to till the land again and sow crops for the winter months. There were cattle fairs and wrestling matches. The days were warm and sultry. The water in the river was no longer muddy, and one evening Grandfather brought home a huge mahseer fish and Sita made it into a delicious curry.

~

Grandfather sat outside the hut, smoking his hookah. Sita was at the far end of the island, spreading clothes on the rocks to dry. One of the goats had followed her. It was the friendlier of the two, and often followed Sita about the island. She had made it a necklace of coloured beads.

She sat down on a smooth rock, and, as she did so, she noticed a small bright object in the sand near her feet. She stooped and picked it up. It was a little wooden toy—a coloured peacock—that must have come down on the river and been swept ashore on the island. Some of the paint had rubbed off, but for Sita, who had no toys, it was a great find. Perhaps it would speak to her, as Mumta had spoken to her.

As she held the toy peacock in the palm of her hand, she thought she heard the flute music again, but she did not look up. She had heard it before, and she was sure that it was all in her mind.

But this time the music sounded nearer, much nearer. There was a soft footfall in the sand. And, looking up, she saw the boy Krishan standing over her.

'I thought you would never come,' said Sita.

'I had to wait until the rains were over. Now that I am free, I will come more often. Did you keep my flute?'

'Yes, but I cannot play it properly. Sometimes it plays by itself, I think, but it will not play for me!'

'I will teach you to play it,' said Krishan.

He sat down beside her, and they cooled their feet in the water, which was clear now, reflecting the blue of the sky.

You could see the sand and the pebbles of the riverbed.

'Sometimes the river is angry, and sometimes it is kind,' said Sita.

'We are part of the river,' said the boy. 'We cannot live without it.'

It was a good river, deep and strong, beginning in the mountains and ending in the sea. Along its banks, for hundreds of miles, lived millions of people, and Sita was only one small girl among them, and no one had ever heard of her, no one knew her—except for the old man, the boy and the river.

A TIGER IN THE HOUSE

❧

Timothy, the tiger cub, was discovered by Grandfather on a hunting expedition in the Terai jungle near Dehra.

Grandfather was no shikari, but as he knew the forests of the Siwalik hills better than most people, he was persuaded to accompany the party—it consisted of several Very Important Persons from Delhi—to advise on the terrain and the direction the beaters should take once a tiger had been spotted.

The camp itself was sumptuous—seven large tents (one for each shikari), a dining tent and a number of servants' tents. The dinner was very good—as Grandfather admitted afterwards, it was not often that one saw hot water plates, finger glasses and seven or eight courses in a tent in the jungle! But that was how things were done in the days of the Viceroys... There were also some fifteen elephants, four of them with howdahs for the shikaris, and the others specially trained for taking part in the beat.

The sportsmen never saw a tiger, nor did they shoot anything else, though they saw a number of deer, peacock and wild boar. They were giving up all hope of finding a tiger and were beginning to shoot at jackals, when Grandfather, strolling down the forest path at some distance from the rest of the party, discovered a little tiger about eighteen inches long, hiding among the intricate roots of a banyan tree. Grandfather picked him up and brought him home after the camp had broken up. He had the distinction of being the only member of the party to have bagged any game, dead or alive.

At first the tiger cub, who was named Timothy by Grandmother, was brought up entirely on milk given to him in a feeding bottle by our cook, Mehmoud. But the milk proved too rich for him, and he was put on a diet of raw mutton and cod liver oil, to be followed later by a more tempting diet of pigeons and rabbits.

Timothy was provided with two companions—Toto the monkey, who was bold enough to pull the young tiger by the tail, and then climb up the curtains if Timothy lost his temper; and a small mongrel puppy, found on the road by Grandfather.

At first, Timothy appeared to be quite afraid of the puppy and darted back with a spring if it came too near. He would make absurd dashes at it with his large forepaws and then retreat to a ridiculously safe distance. Finally, he allowed the puppy to crawl on his back and rest there!

One of Timothy's favourite amusements was to stalk anyone who would play with him, and so, when I came to live with Grandfather, I became one of the tiger's favourites.

With a crafty look in his glittering eyes, and his body crouching, he would creep closer and closer to me, suddenly making a dash for my feet, rolling over on his back and kicking with delight, and pretending to bite my ankles.

He was by this time the size of a full-grown retriever, and when I took him out for walks, people on the road would give us a wide berth. When he pulled hard on his chain, I had difficulty in keeping up with him. His favourite place in the house was the drawing room, and he would make himself comfortable on the long sofa, reclining there with great dignity and snarling at anybody who tried to get him off.

Timothy had clean habits, and would scrub his face with his paws exactly like a cat. He slept at night in the cook's quarters, and was always delighted at being let out by him in the morning.

'One of these days,' declared Grandmother in her prophetic manner, 'we are going to find Timothy sitting on Mehmoud's bed, and no sign of the cook except his clothes and shoes!'

Of course, it never came to that, but when Timothy was about six months old, a change came over him; he grew steadily less friendly. When out for a walk with me, he would try to steal away to stalk a cat or someone's pet Pekinese. Sometimes at night we would hear frenzied cackling from the poultry house, and in the morning there would be feathers lying all over the veranda. Timothy had to be chained up more often. And, finally, when he began to stalk Mehmoud about the house with what looked like villainous intent, Grandfather decided it was time to transfer him to a zoo.

The nearest zoo was at Lucknow, two hundred miles away.

Reserving a first-class compartment for himself and Timothy—no one would share a compartment with them—Grandfather took him to Lucknow where the zoo authorities were only too glad to receive as a gift a well-fed and fairly civilized tiger.

About six months later, when my grandparents were visiting relatives in Lucknow, Grandfather took the opportunity of calling at the zoo to see how Timothy was getting on. I was not there to accompany him, but I heard all about it when he returned to Dehra.

Arriving at the zoo, Grandfather made straight for the particular cage in which Timothy had been interned. The tiger was there, crouched in a corner, full-grown and with a magnificent striped coat.

'Hello, Timothy!' said Grandfather and, climbing the railing with ease, he put his arm through the bars of the cage.

The tiger approached the bars and allowed Grandfather to put both hands around his head. Grandfather stroked the tiger's forehead and tickled his ear, and, whenever he growled, smacked him across the mouth, which was his old way of keeping him quiet.

He licked Grandfather's hands and only sprang away when a leopard in the next cage snarled at him. Grandfather 'shooed' the leopard away and the tiger returned to lick his hands; but every now and then the leopard would rush at the bars and the tiger would slink back to his corner.

A number of people had gathered to watch the reunion when a keeper pushed his way through the crowd and asked Grandfather what he was doing.

'I'm talking to Timothy,' said Grandfather. 'Weren't you here when I gave him to the zoo six months ago?'

'I haven't been here very long,' said the surprised keeper. 'Please continue your conversation. But I have never been able to touch him myself, he is always very bad tempered.'

'Why don't you put him somewhere else?' suggested Grandfather. 'That leopard keeps frightening him. I'll go and see the superintendent about it.'

Grandfather went in search of the superintendent of the zoo, but found that he had gone home early; and so, after wandering about the zoo for a little while, he returned to Timothy's cage to say goodbye. It was beginning to get dark.

He had been stroking and slapping Timothy for about five minutes when he found another keeper observing him with some alarm. Grandfather recognized him as the keeper who had been there when Timothy had first come to the zoo.

'*You* remember me,' said Grandfather. 'Now why don't you transfer Timothy to another cage, away from this stupid leopard?'

'But—sir—' stammered the keeper, 'it is not your tiger.'

'I know, I know,' said Grandfather testily. 'I realize he is no longer mine. But you might at least take a suggestion or two from me.'

'I remember your tiger very well,' said the keeper. 'He died two months ago.'

'Died!' exclaimed Grandfather.

'Yes, sir, of pneumonia. This tiger was trapped in the hills only last month, and he is very dangerous!'

Grandfather could think of nothing to say. The tiger was

still licking his arm, with increasing relish. Grandfather took what seemed to him an age to withdraw his hand from the cage.

With his face near the tiger's he mumbled, 'Goodnight, Timothy,' and giving the keeper a scornful look, walked briskly out of the zoo.

LISTEN!

~

Listen to the night wind in the trees,
Listen to the summer grass singing;
Listen to the time that's tripping by,
And the dawn dew falling.
Listen to the moon as it climbs the sky,
Listen to the pebbles humming;
Listen to the mist in the trembling leaves,
And the silence calling.

THE GLACIER

~

It was a fine sunny morning when we set out to cover the last seven miles to the glacier. We had expected this to be a stiff climb, but the last dak bungalow was situated at well over 10,000 feet above sea level, and the ascent was to be fairly gradual.

And then suddenly, abruptly, there were no more trees. As the bungalow dropped out of sight, the trees and bushes gave way to short grass and little blue and pink alpine flowers. The snow peaks were close now, ringing us in on every side. We passed waterfalls, cascading hundreds of feet down precipitous rock faces, thundering into the little river. A great golden eagle hovered over us for some time.

'I feel different again,' said Kamal.

'We're very high now,' I said. 'I hope we won't get headaches.'

'I've got one already,' complained Anil. 'Let's have some tea.'

We had left our cooking utensils at the bungalow, expecting to return there for the night, and had brought with us only a few biscuits, chocolate, and a thermos of tea. We finished the tea, and Bisnu scrambled about on the grassy slopes, collecting wild strawberries. They were tiny strawberries, very sweet, and they did nothing to satisfy our appetites. There was no sign of habitation or human life. The only creatures to be found at that height were the gurals—sure-footed mountain goats—and an occasional snow leopard, or a bear.

We found and explored a small cave and then, turning a bend, came unexpectedly upon the glacier.

The hill fell away and there, confronting us, was a great white field of snow and ice, cradled between two peaks that could only have been the abode of the gods. We were speechless for several minutes. Kamal took my hand and held on to it for reassurance; perhaps he was not sure that what he saw was real. Anil's mouth hung open. Bisnu's eyes glittered with excitement.

We proceeded cautiously on the snow, supporting each other on the slippery surface, but we could not go far, because we were quite unequipped for any high-altitude climbing. It was pleasant to feel that we were the only boys in our town who had climbed so high. A few black rocks jutted out from the snow, and we sat down on them to feast our eyes on the view. The sun reflected sharply from the snow and we felt surprisingly warm.

'Let's sunbathe!' said Anil, on a sudden impulse.

'Yes, let's do that!' I said.

In a few minutes we had taken off our clothes and, sitting

on the rocks, were exposing ourselves to the elements. It was delicious to feel the sun crawling over my skin. Within half an hour I was a post-box red, and so was Bisnu, and the two of us decided to get into our clothes before the sun scorched the skin off our backs. Kamal and Anil appeared to be more resilient to sunlight and laughed at our discomfiture. Bisnu and I avenged ourselves by gathering up handfuls of snow and rubbing it on their backs. They dressed quickly enough after that, Anil leaping about like a performing monkey.

Meanwhile, almost imperceptibly, clouds had covered some of the peaks, and a white mist drifted down the mountain slopes. It was time to get back to the bungalow; we would barely make it before dark.

We had not gone far when lightning began to sizzle above the mountain tops, followed by waves of thunder.

'Let's run!' shouted Anil. 'We can take shelter in the cave!'

The clouds could hold themselves in no longer, and the rain came down suddenly, stinging our faces as it was whipped up by an icy wind. Half-blinded, we ran as fast as we could along the slippery path and stumbled, drenched and exhausted, into the little cave.

The cave was mercifully dry and not very dark We remained at the entrance, watching the rain sweep past us, listening to the wind whistling down the long gorge.

'It will take some time to stop,' said Kamal.

'No, it will pass soon,' said Bisnu. 'These storms are short and fierce.'

Anil produced his pocket knife and, to pass the time, we carved our names in the smooth rock of the cave.

'We will come here again, when we are older,' said Kamal, 'and perhaps our names will still be here.'

It had grown dark by the time the rain stopped. A full moon helped us find our way. We went slowly and carefully. The rain had loosened the earth and stones kept rolling down the hillside. I was afraid of starting a landslide.

'I hope we don't meet the Lidini now,' said Anil fervently.

'I thought you didn't believe in her,' I said.

'I don't,' replied Anil. 'But what if I'm wrong?'

We saw only a gural, poised on the brow of a precipice, silhouetted against the sky.

And then the path vanished.

Had it not been for the bright moonlight, we might have walked straight into an empty void. The rain had caused a landslide and where there had been a narrow path there was now only a precipice of loose, slippery shale.

'We'll have to go back,' said Bisnu. 'It will be too dangerous to try and cross in the dark.'

'We'll sleep in the cave,' I suggested.

'We've nothing to sleep in,' said Anil. 'Not a single blanket between us—and nothing to eat!'

'We'll just have to rough it till morning,' said Kamal. 'It will be better than breaking our necks here.'

We returned to the cave, which did, at least, have the virtue of being dry. Bisnu had matches and he made a fire with some dry sticks which had been left in the cave by a previous party. We ate what was left of a loaf of bread.

There was no sleep for any of us that night. We lay close to each other for comfort, but the ground was hard and uneven. And every noise we heard outside the cave made us think of leopards and bears and even Abominable Snowmen.

We got up as soon as there was a faint glow in the sky. The snow peaks were bright pink, but we were too tired and hungry and worried to care for the beauty of the sunrise. We took the path to the landslide and once again looked for a way across. Kamal ventured to take a few steps on the loose pebbles, but the ground gave way immediately and we had to grab him by the arms and shoulder to prevent him from sliding a hundred feet down the gorge.

'Now what are we going to do?' I asked,

'Look for another way,' said Bisnu.

'But do you know of any?'

And we all turned to look at Bisnu, expecting him to provide the solution to our problem.

'I have heard of a way,' said Bisnu, 'but I have never used it. It will be a little dangerous, I think. The path has not been used for several years—not since the traders stopped coming in from Tibet.'

'Never mind, we'll try it,' said Anil.

'We will have to cross the glacier first,' said Bisnu. 'That's the main problem.'

We looked at each other in silence. The glacier didn't look difficult to cross, but we knew that it would not be easy for novices like us. For almost a quarter of a mile it consisted of hard, slippery ice.

Anil was the first to arrive at a decision.

'Come on,' he said. 'There's no time to waste.'

We were soon on the glacier. And we remained on it for

a long time. For every two steps forward, we slid one step backward. Our progress was slow and awkward. Sometimes, after advancing several yards across the ice at a steep incline, one of us should slip back and the others would have to slither down to help him up. At one particularly difficult spot, I dropped our water bottle and, grabbing at it, lost my footing, fell full-length and went sliding some twenty feet down the ice slope.

I had sprained my wrist and hurt my knee, and was to prove a liability for the rest of the trek.

Kamal tied his handkerchief round my hand, and Anil took charge of the water bottle, which we had filled with ice. Using my good hand to grab Bisnu's legs whenever I slipped, I struggled on behind the others.

It was almost noon, and we were quite famished, when we put our feet on grass again. And then we had another steep climb, clutching at roots and grasses, before we reached the path that Bisnu had spoken about. It was little more than a goat track, but it took us round the mountain and brought us within sight of the dak bungalow.

'I could eat a whole chicken,' said Kamal.

'I could eat two,' I said.

'I could eat a Snowman,' said Bisnu.

'And I could eat the chowkidar,' said Anil.

Fortunately for the chowkidar, he had anticipated our hunger, and when we staggered into the bungalow late in the afternoon, we found a meal waiting for us. True, there was no chicken but so ravenous did we feel, that even the lowly onion tasted delicious!

We had Bisnu to thank for getting us back successfully. He had brought us over mountain and glacier with all the skill and confidence of a boy who had the Himalayas in his blood.

We took our time getting back to Kapkote, fished in the Sarayu river, bathed with the village boys we had seen on our way up, collected strawberries and ferns and wild flowers, and finally said goodbye to Bisnu.

Anil wanted to take Bisnu along with us, but the boy's parents refused to let him go, saying that he was too young for the life in a city; but we were of the opinion that Bisnu could have taught the city boys a few things.

'Never mind,' said Kamal. 'We'll go on another trip next year and we'll take you with us, Bisnu. We'll write and let you know our plans.'

This promise made Bisnu happy and he saw us off at the bus stop, shouldering our bedding to the end. Then he skimmed up the trunk of a fir tree to have a better view of us leaving and we saw him waving to us from the tree as our bus went round the bend from Kapkote, and the hills were left behind and the plains stretched out below.

TO SEE A TIGER

~

Mr Kishore drove me out to the forest rest house in his jeep, told me he'd be back in two days, and left me in the jungle. The caretaker of the rest house, a retired Indian Army corporal, made me a cup of tea.

'You have come to see the animals, sir?'

'Yes,' I said, looking around the clearing in front of the house, where a few domestic fowls scrabbled in the dust. 'Will I have to go far?'

'This is the best place, sir,' said the caretaker. 'See, the river is just below.'

A stream of clear mountain water ran through a shady glade of sal and sheesham trees about fifty yards from the house.

'The animals come at night,' said the caretaker. 'You can sit in the veranda with a cup of tea, and watch them. You must be very quiet, of course.'

'Will I see a tiger?' I asked. 'I've *come* to see a tiger.'

'Perhaps the tiger will come, sir,' said the caretaker with a tolerant smile. 'He will do his best, I am sure.'

He made me a simple lunch of rice and lentils, flavoured with a mango pickle. I spent the afternoon with a book taken from the rest house bookshelf. The small library hadn't been touched for over twenty years, and I had to make my choice from Marie Corelli, P.C. Wren, and early Wodehouse. I plumped for a Wodehouse—*Love Among the Chickens*. A peacock flaunted its tail feathers on the lawn, but I was not distracted. I had seen plenty of peacocks.

When it grew dark, I took up my position in the veranda, on an old cane chair. Bhag Singh, the caretaker, brought me dinner on a brass thali, with two different vegetables in separate katoris. The chapattis came in relays, brought hot from the kitchen by Bhag Singh's ten-year-old son. Then, sustained by more tea, sweet and milky, I began my vigil. It took an hour for Bhag Singh's family to settle down for the night in their outhouse. Their pi-dog stood outside, barking at me for half an hour, before he, too, fell asleep. The moon came up over the foothills, and the stream could be seen quite clearly.

And then a strange sound filled the night air. Not the roar of a tiger, nor the sawing of a leopard, but a rising crescendo of noise—wurk, wurk, wurk—issuing from the muddy banks near the stream. All the frogs in the jungle seemed to have gathered there that night. They must have been having a sort of Old Boys' Reunion, because everyone seemed to have something to say for himself. The speeches continued for about an hour. Then the meeting broke up, and silence returned to the forest.

A jackal slunk across the clearing. A puff of wind brushed through the trees. I was almost asleep when a cicada burst into violent music in a nearby tree. I started, and stared out at the silver, moon-green stream; but no animals came to drink that night. The next evening, Bhag Singh offered to sit up with me. He placed a charcoal burner on the veranda, and topped it with a large basin of tea.

'Whenever you feel sleepy, sir, I'll give you a glass of tea.'

Did we hear a panther—or was it someone sawing wood? The sounds are similar, in the distance. The frogs started up again. The Old Boys must have brought their wives along this time, because instead of speeches there was general conversation, exactly like the natter of a cocktail party.

By morning I had drunk over fifteen cups of tea. Out of respect for my grandfather, a pioneer tea planter in India, I did not complain. Bhag Singh made me an English breakfast— toast, fried eggs and more tea.

The third night passed in much the same way, except that Bhag Singh's son stayed up with us and drank his quota of tea.

In the morning, Mr Kishore came for me in his jeep.

'Did you see anything?'

'A jackal,' I said.

'Never mind, you'll have better luck next time. Of course, the jungles aren't what they used to be.'

I said goodbye to Bhag Singh, and got into the jeep.

We had gone barely a hundred yards along the forest road when Mr Kishore brought the jeep to a sudden, jolting halt.

Right in the middle of the road, about thirty yards in front of us, stood a magnificent full-grown tiger.

The tiger didn't roar. He didn't even snarl. But he gave us what appeared to be a quick, disdainful glance, and then walked majestically across the road and into the jungle.

'What luck!' exclaimed Mr Kishore. 'You can't complain now, can you? You've seen your tiger!'

'Yes,' I said. 'three sleepless nights, and I've seen it in broad daylight!'

'Never mind,' said Mr Kishore. 'If you're tired, I know just the thing for you—a nice cup of tea.'

I think it was Malcolm Muggeridge who said that the only real Englishmen left in the world were to be found in India.

GUESTS WHO COME IN
FROM THE FOREST

~

When mist fills the Himalayan valleys, and heavy monsoon rain sweeps across the hills, it is natural for wild creatures to seek shelter. Any shelter is welcome in a storm—and sometimes my cottage in the forest is the most convenient refuge.

There is no doubt that I make things easier for all concerned by leaving most of my windows open. I am one of those peculiar people who like to have plenty of fresh air indoors—and if a few birds, beasts and insects come in too, they're welcome, provided they don't make too much of a nuisance of themselves.

I must confess that I did lose patience with a bamboo beetle who blundered in the other night and fell into the water jug. I rescued him and pushed him out of the window. A few seconds later he came whirring in again, and with unerring accuracy landed with a plop in the same jug. I fished him out once more and offered him the freedom of the night. But attracted no doubt by the light and warmth of my small sitting room, he came buzzing back, circling the room like a helicopter, looking for a good place to land. Quickly I covered the water jug. He landed in a bowl of wild dahlias, and I allowed him to remain there, comfortably curled up in the hollow of a flower.

Sometimes, during the day, a bird visits me—a deep purple whistling thrush, hopping about on long dainty legs, peering to the right and left, too nervous to sing. She perches on the windowsill, looking out at the rain. She does not permit any familiarity. But if I sit quietly in my chair, she will sit quietly on her windowsill, glancing quickly at me now and then just to make sure that I'm keeping my distance. When the rain stops, she glides away, and it is only then, confident in her freedom, that she bursts into full-throated song, her broken but haunting melody echoing down the ravine.

A squirrel comes sometimes; when his home in the oak tree gets waterlogged. Apparently he is a bachelor; anyway, he lives alone. He knows me well, this squirrel, and is bold enough to climb on to the dining table looking for tidbits which he always finds, because I leave them there deliberately. Had I met him when he was a youngster, he would have learnt to eat from my hand, but I have only been here a few months. I like it this way. I am not looking for pets: these are simply guests.

Last week, as I was sitting down at my desk to write a

long-deferred article, I was startled to see an emerald-green praying mantis sitting on my writing pad. He peered up at me with his protuberant glass-bead eyes; and I stared down at him through my reading glasses. When I gave him a prod, he moved off in a leisurely way. Later I found him examining the binding of Whitman's *Leaves of Grass;* perhaps he had found a succulent bookworm. He disappeared for a couple of days, and then I found him again on the dressing table, preening himself before the mirror. Perhaps I am doing him an injustice in assuming that he was preening. Maybe he thought he'd met another mantis and was simply trying to make contact. Anyway, he seemed fascinated by his reflection.

Out in the garden, I spotted another mantis, perched on the jasmine bush. Its arms were raised like a boxer's. Perhaps they're a pair, I thought, and went indoors and fetched my mantis and placed him on the jasmine bush, opposite his fellow insect. He did not like what he saw—no comparison with his own image!—and made off in a huff.

My most interesting visitor comes at night, when the lights are still burning—a tiny bat who prefers to fly in at the door, should it be open, and will use the window only if there's no alternative. His object in entering the house is to snap up the moths that cluster around the lamps.

All the bats I've seen fly fairly high, keeping near the ceiling as far as possible, and only descending to ear level (my ear level) when they must; but this particular bat flies in low, like a dive bomber, and does acrobatics amongst the furniture, zooming in and out of chair legs and under tables. Once, while careening about the room in this fashion, he passed straight between my legs.

Has his radar gone wrong, I wondered, or is he just plain crazy?

I went to my shelves of *Natural History* and looked up bats, but could find no explanation for this erratic behaviour. As a last resort, I turned to an ancient volume, Sterndale's *Indian Mammalia* (Calcutta, 1884), and in it, to my delight, I found what I was looking for:

> a bat found near Mussoorie by Captain Hutton, on the southern range of hills at 5500 feet; head and body, 1.4 inch; skims close to the ground, instead of flying high as bats generally do; habitat, Jharipani, N.W. Himalayas.

Apparently the bat was rare even in 1884.

Perhaps I've come across one of the few surviving members of the species: Jharipani is only two miles from where I live. And I feel rather offended that modern authorities should have ignored this tiny bat; possibly they feel that it is already extinct. If so, I'm pleased to have rediscovered it. I am happy that it survives in my small corner of the woods, and I undertake to celebrate it in verse:

Most bats fly high,
Swooping only
To take some insect on the wing;
But there's a bat I know
Who flies so low
He skims the floor.

He does not enter at the window
But flies in at the door,
Does stunts beneath the furniture—
Is his radar wrong,
Or does he just prefer
Being different from other bats?
And when sometimes
He settles upside down
At the foot of my bed, I let him be.
On lonely nights, even a crazy bat
Is company.

TIGER, TIGER, BURNING BRIGHT

~

On the left bank of the Ganga, where it emerges from the Himalayan foothills, there is a long stretch of heavy forest. These are villages on the fringe of the forest, inhabited by bamboo cutters and farmers, but there are few signs of commerce or pilgrimage. Hunters, however, have found the area an ideal hunting ground during the last seventy years, and as a result the animals are not as numerous as they used to be. The trees, too, have been disappearing slowly; and, as the forest recedes, the animals lose their food and shelter and move on further into the foothills. Slowly, they are being denied the right to live.

Only the elephant can cross the river. And two years ago, when a large area of the forest was cleared to make way for a refugee resettlement camp, a herd of elephants—finding their favourite food, the green shoots of the bamboo, in short supply—waded across the river. They crashed through the suburbs of Haridwar, knocked down a factory wall, pulled down several tin roofs, held up a train, and left a trail of devastation in their wake until they found a new home in a new forest which was still untouched. Here, they settled down to a new life—but an unsettled, wary life. They did not know when men would appear again, with tractors, bulldozers and dynamite.

There was a time when the forest on the banks of the Ganga had provided food and shelter for some thirty or forty tigers; but men in search of trophies had shot them all, and now there remained only one old tiger in the jungle. Many hunters had tried to get him, but he was a wise and crafty old tiger, who knew the ways of men, and he had so far survived all attempts on his life.

Although the tiger had passed the prime of his life, he had lost none of his majesty. His muscles rippled beneath the golden yellow of his coat, and he walked through the long grass with the confidence of one who knew that he was still a king, even though his subjects were fewer. His great head pushed through the foliage, and it was only his tail, swinging high, that showed occasionally above the sea of grass.

In late spring he would head for the large jheel, the only water in the forest (if you don't count the river, which was several miles away), which was almost a lake during the rainy season, but just a muddy marsh at this time of the year.

Here, at different times of the day and night, all the animals came to drink—the long-horned sambhar, the delicate chital, the swamp deer, the hyenas and jackals, the wild boar, the panthers—and the lone tiger. Since the elephants had gone, the water was usually clear except when buffaloes from the nearest village came to wallow in it, and then it was very muddy. These buffaloes, though they were not wild, were not afraid of the panther or even of the tiger. They knew the panther was afraid of their massive horns and that the tiger preferred the flesh of the deer.

One day, there were several sambhars at the water's edge; but they did not stay long. The scent of the tiger came with the breeze, and there was no mistaking its strong feline odour. The deer held their heads high for a few moments, their nostrils twitching, and then scattered into the forest, disappearing behind a screen of leaf and bamboo.

When the tiger arrived, there was no other animal near the water. But the birds were still there. The egrets continued to wade in the shallows, and a kingfisher darted low over the water, dived suddenly—a flash of blue and gold—and made off with a slim silver fish, which glistened in the sun like a polished gem. A long brown snake glided in and out among the waterlilies and disappeared beneath a fallen tree which lay rotting in the shallows.

The tiger waited in the shelter of a rock, his ears pricked up for the least unfamiliar sound; he knew that it was at that place that men sometimes sat up for him with guns, for they coveted his beauty—his stripes, and the gold of his body, his fine teeth, his whiskers and his noble head. They would have liked to hang his skin on a wall, with his head stuffed and mounted, and pieces of glass replacing his fierce eyes. Then they would have boasted of their triumph over the king of the jungle.

The tiger had encountered hunters before, so he did not usually show himself in the open during the day. But of late he had heard no guns, and if there were hunters around, you would have heard their guns (for a man with a gun cannot resist letting it off, even if it is only at a rabbit—or at another man). And, besides, the tiger was thirsty.

He was also feeling quite hot. It was March, and the shimmering dust haze of summer had come early. Tigers—unlike other cats—are fond of water, and on a hot day will wallow in it for hours.

He walked into the water, in amongst the water lilies, and drank slowly. He was seldom in a hurry when he ate or drank. Other animals might bolt down their food, but they are only other animals. A tiger is a tiger; he has his dignity to preserve even though he isn't aware of it!

He raised his head and listened, one paw suspended in the air. A strange sound had come to him on the breeze, and he was wary of strange sounds. So he moved swiftly into the shelter of the tall grass that bordered the jheel, and climbed a hillock until he reached his favourite rock. This rock was big enough both to hide him and to give him shade. Anyone looking up from the jheel would have thought it strange that the rock had a round bump on the top. The bump was the tiger's head. He kept it very still.

The sound he heard was only the sound of a flute, rendered thin and reedy in the forest. It belonged to Ramu, a slim brown boy who rode a buffalo. Ramu played vigorously on the flute. Shyam, a slightly smaller boy, riding another buffalo, brought up the rear of the herd.

There were about eight buffaloes in the herd, and they belonged to the families of the two friends Ramu and Shyam. Their people were Gujars, a nomadic community who earned a livelihood by keeping buffaloes and selling milk and butter. The boys were about twelve years old, but they could not have told you exactly, because in their village nobody thought birthdays were important. They were almost the same age as the tiger, but he was old and experienced while they were still cubs.

The tiger had often seen them at the jheel, and he was not worried by their presence. He knew the village people would do him no harm as long as he left their buffaloes alone. Once, when he was younger and full of bravado, he had killed a buffalo—not because he was hungry, but because he was young and wanted to try out his strength—and after that the villagers had hunted him for days, with spears, bows and an old muzzleloader. Now he left the buffaloes alone, even though the deer in the forest were not as numerous as before.

The boys knew that a tiger lived in the jungle, for they had often heard him roar; but they did not suspect that he was so near just then.

The tiger gazed down from his rock, and the sight of eight fat black buffaloes made him give a low, throaty moan. But the boys were there. Besides, a buffalo was not easy to kill.

He decided to move on and find a cool shady place in the heart of the jungle where he could rest during the warm afternoon and be free of the flies and mosquitoes that swarmed around the jheel. At night he would hunt.

With a lazy, half-humorous roar—'A-oonh!'—he got up

off his haunches and sauntered off into the jungle.

Even the gentlest of the tiger's roars can be heard half a mile away, and the boys, who were barely fifty yards away, looked up immediately.

'There he goes!' said Ramu, taking the flute from his lips and pointing it towards the hillocks. He was not afraid, for he knew that this tiger was not interested in humans. 'Did you see him?'

'I saw his tail, just before he disappeared. He's a big tiger!'

'Do not call him tiger. Call him uncle, or maharaja.'

'Oh, why?'

'Don't you know that it's unlucky to call a tiger a tiger? My father always told me so. If you meet a tiger, and call him uncle, he will leave you alone.'

'I'll try and remember that,' said Shyam.

The buffaloes were now well inside the water, and some of them were lying down in the mud. Buffaloes love soft wet mud and will wallow in it for hours. The slushier the mud the better. Ramu, to avoid being dragged down into the mud with his buffalo, slipped off its back and plunged into the water. He waded to a small islet covered with reeds and water lilies. Shyam was close behind him.

They lay down on their hard flat stomachs, on a patch of grass, and allowed the warm sun to beat down on their bare brown bodies.

Ramu was the more knowledgeable boy because he had been to Hardiwar and Dehradun several times with his father. Shyam had never been out of the village.

Shyam said, 'The pool is not so deep this year.'

'We have had no rain since January,' said Ramu. 'If we do not get rain soon the jheel may dry up altogether.'

'And then what will we do?'

'We? I don't know. There is a well in the village. But even that may dry up. My father told me that it did once, just about the time I was born, and everyone had to walk ten miles to the river for water.'

'And what about the animals?'

'Some will stay here and die. Others will go to the river. But there are too many people near the river now—and temples, houses and factories—so the animals stay away. And the trees have been cut, so that between the jungle and the river there is no place to hide. Animals are afraid of the open—they are afraid of men with guns.'

'Even at night?'

'At night men come in jeeps, with searchlights. They kill the deer for meat, and sell the skins of tigers and panthers.'

'I didn't know a tiger's skin was worth anything.'

'It's worth more than our skins,' said Ramu knowingly. 'It will fetch six hundred rupees. Who would pay that much for one of us?'

'Our fathers would.'

'True—if they had the money.'

'If my father sold his fields, he would get more than six hundred rupees.'

'True—but if he sold his fields, none of you would have anything to eat. A man needs land as much as a tiger needs a jungle.'

'Yes,' said Shyam. 'And that reminds me—my mother

asked me to take some roots home.'

'I will help you.'

They walked deeper into the jheel until the water was up to their waists, and began pulling up water lilies by the roots. The flower is beautiful, but the villagers value the root more. When it is cooked, it makes a delicious and nourishing dish. The plant multiples rapidly and is aways in good supply. In the year when famine hit the village, it was only the root of the water lily that saved many from starvation.

When Shyam and Ramu had finished gathering roots, they emerged from the water and passed the time wrestling with each other, slipping about in the soft mud, which soon covered them from head to toe.

To get rid of the mud, they dived into the water again and swam across to their buffaloes. Then, jumping on to their backs and digging their heels into the thick hides, the boys raced them across the jheel, shouting and hollering so much that all the birds flew away in fright, and the monkeys set up a shrill chattering of their own in the dhak trees. In March, the flame of the forest, or dhak trees, are ablaze with bright scarlet and orange flowers.

It was evening, and the twilight was fading fast, when the buffalo herd finally wandered its way homeward, to be greeted outside the village by the barking of dogs, the gurgle of hookah pipes, and the homely smell of cow-dung smoke.

∼

The tiger made a kill that night—a chital. He made his approach against the wind so that the unsuspecting spotted deer did not see him until it was too late. A blow on the deer's haunches from the tiger's paw brought it down, and then the great beast fastened his fangs on the deer's throat. It was all over in a few minutes. The tiger was too quick and strong, and the deer did not struggle much.

It was a violent end for so gentle a creature. But you must not imagine that in the jungle the deer live in permanent fear of death. It is only man, with his imagination and his fear of the hereafter, who is afraid of dying. In the jungle it is different. Sudden death appears at intervals. Wild creatures do not have to think about it, and so the sudden killing of one of their number by some predator of the forest is only a fleeting incident soon forgotten by the survivors.

The tiger feasted well, growling with pleasure as he ate his way up the body, leaving the entrails. When he had had his night's fill, he left the carcass for the vultures and jackals. The cunning old tiger never returned to the same carcass, even if there was still plenty left to eat. In the past, when he had gone back to a kill, he had often found a man sitting in a tree waiting for him with a rifle.

His belly filled, the tiger sauntered over to the edge of the forest and looked out across the sandy wasteland and the deep, singing river, at the twinkling lights of Rishikesh on the opposite bank, and raised his head and roared his defiance at mankind.

He was a lonesome bachelor. It was five or six years since he had a mate. She had been shot by the trophy hunters, and her two cubs had been trapped by men who do trade in wild animals. One went to a circus, where he had to learn tricks to amuse men and respond to the crack of a whip; the other, more fortunate, went first to a zoo in Delhi and was later transferred to a zoo in America.

Sometimes, when the old tiger was very lonely, he gave a great roar, which could be heard throughout the forest. The villagers thought he was roaring in anger, but the jungle knew that he was really roaring out of loneliness. When the sound of his roar had died away, he paused, standing still, waiting for an answering roar; but it never came. It was taken up instead by the shrill scream of a barbet high up in a sal tree.

It was dawn now, dew-fresh and cool, and the jungle dwellers were on the move. The black beady little eyes of a jungle rat were fixed on a brown hen who was pecking around in the undergrowth near her nest. He had a large family to feed, this rat, and he knew that in the hen's nest was a clutch of delicious fawn-coloured eggs. He waited patiently for nearly an hour before he had the satisfaction of seeing the hen leave her nest and go off in search of food.

As soon as she had gone, the rat lost no time in making his raid. Slipping quietly out of his hole, he slithered along among the leaves; but, clever as he was, he did not realize that his own movements were being watched.

A pair of grey mongooses scouted about in the dry grass. They, too, were hungry, and eggs usually figured large on their menu. Now, lying still on an outcrop of rock, they watched the rat sneaking along, occasionally sniffing at the air and finally vanishing behind a boulder. When he reappeared, he was struggling to roll an egg uphill towards his hole.

The rat was in difficulty, pushing the egg sometimes with

his paws, sometimes with his nose. The ground was rough, and the egg wouldn't move straight. Deciding that he must have help, he scuttled off to call his spouse. Even now the mongooses did not descend on the tantalizing egg. They waited until the rat returned with his wife, and then watched as the male rat took the egg firmly between his forepaws and rolled over on to his back. The female rat then grabbed her mate's tail and began to drag him along.

Totally absorbed in the struggle with the egg, the rat did not hear the approach of the mongooses. When these two large furry visitors suddenly bobbed up from behind a stone, the rats squealed with fright, abandoned the egg, and fled for their lives.

The mongooses wasted no time in breaking open the egg and making a meal of it. But just as, a few minutes ago, the rat had not noticed their approach, so now they did not notice the village boy, carrying a small bright axe and a net bag in his hands, creeping along.

Ramu, too, was searching for eggs, and when he saw the mongooses busy with one, he stood still to watch them, his eyes roving in search of the nest. He was hoping the mongooses would lead him to the nest; but, when they had finished their meal and made off into the undergrowth, Ramu had to do his own searching. He failed to find the nest, and moved further into the forest. The rat's hopes were just reviving when, to his disgust, the mother hen returned.

Ramu now made his way to a mahua tree.

The flowers of the mahua can be eaten by animals as well as by men. Bears are particularly fond of them and will eat large quantities of flowers, which gradually start fermenting in their stomachs with the result that the animals get quite drunk. Ramu had often seen a couple of bears stumbling home to their cave, bumping into each other or into the trunks of trees. They are short-sighted to begin with, and when drunk can hardly see at all. But their sense of smell and hearing are so good that in the end they find their way home.

Ramu decided he would gather some mahua flowers, and climbed up the tree, which is leafless when it blossoms. He began breaking the white flowers and throwing them to the ground. He had been on the tree for about five minutes when he heard the whining grumble of a bear, and presently a young sloth bear ambled into the clearing beneath the tree.

He was a small bear, little more than a cub, and Ramu was not frightened; but, because he thought the mother might be in the vicinity, he decided to take no chances, and sat very still, waiting to see what the bear would do. He hoped it wouldn't choose the mahua tree for a meal.

At first, the young bear put his nose to the ground and sniffed his way along until he came to a large anthill. Here he began huffing and puffing, blowing rapidly in and out of his nostrils, causing the dust from the anthill to fly in all directions. But he was a disappointed bear, because the anthill had been deserted long ago. And so, grumbling, he made his way across to a tall wild plum tree, and shinning rapidly up the smooth trunk, was soon perched on its topmost branches. It was only then that he saw Ramu.

The bear at once scrambled several feet higher up the tree, and laid himself out flat on a branch. It wasn't a very thick branch and left a large expanse of bear showing on either side. The bear tucked his head away behind another branch, and so long as he could not see Ramu, seemed quite satisfied that he was well hidden, though he couldn't help grumbling with anxiety, for a bear, like most animals, is afraid of man.

Bears, however, are also very curious—and curiosity has often led them into trouble. Slowly, inch by inch, the young bear's black snout appeared over the edge of the branch; but as soon as the eyes came into view and met Ramu's, he drew back with a jerk and the head was once more hidden. The bear did this two or three times, and Ramu, highly amused, waited until it wasn't looking, then moved some way down the tree. When the bear looked up again and saw that the boy was missing, he was so pleased with himself that he stretched right across to the next branch, to get a plum. Ramu chose this moment to burst into loud laughter. The startled bear tumbled out of the tree, dropped through the branches for a distance of some fifteen feet, and landed with a thud in a heap of dry leaves.

And then several things happened at almost the same time.

The mother bear came charging into the clearing. Spotting Ramu in the tree, she reared up on her hind legs, grunting fiercely. It was Ramu's turn to be startled. There are few animals more dangerous than a rampaging mother bear, and the boy knew that one blow from her clawed forepaws could rip his skull open.

But before the bear could approach the tree, there was a tremendous roar, and the old tiger bounded into the clearing. He had been asleep in the bushes not far away—he liked a good sleep after a heavy meal—and the noise in the clearing had woken him.

He was in a bad mood, and his loud 'A-oonh!' made his displeasure quite clear. The bears turned and ran from the clearing, the youngster squealing with fright.

The tiger then came into the centre of the clearing, looked up at the trembling boy, and roared again.

Ramu nearly fell out of the tree.

'Good day to you, Uncle,' he stammered, showing his teeth in a nervous grin.

Perhaps this was too much for the tiger. With a low growl, he turned his back on the mahua tree and padded off into the jungle, his tail twitching in disgust.

～

That night, when Ramu told his parents and his grandfather about the tiger and how it had saved him from a female bear, it started a round of tiger stories—about how some of them could be gentlemen, others rogues. Sooner or later the conversation came round to man-eaters, and Grandfather told two stories which he swore were true, although his listeners only half believed him.

The first story concerned the belief that a maneating tiger is guided towards his next victim by the spirit of a human being previously killed and eaten by the tiger. Grandfather said that he actually knew three hunters who sat up in a machan over a human kill, and when the tiger came, the corpse sat up and pointed with his right hand at the men in the tree. The tiger then went away. But the hunters knew he would return, and one man was brave enough to get down from the tree and tie the right arm of the corpse to its side. Later, when the tiger returned, the corpse sat up and this time pointed out the men with his left hand. The enraged tiger sprang into the tree and killed his enemies in the machan.

'And then there was a bania,' said Grandfather, beginning another story, 'who lived in a village in the jungle. He wanted to visit a neighbouring village to collect some money that was owed to him, but as the road lay through heavy forest in which lived a terrible man-eating tiger, he did not know what to do. Finally, he went to a sadhu, who gave him two powders. By eating the first powder he could turn into a huge tiger, capable of dealing with any other tiger in the jungle, and by eating the second he would become a bania again.

'Armed with his two powders, and accompanied by his pretty, young wife, the bania set out on his journey. They had not gone far into the forest when they came upon the man-eater sitting in the middle of the road. Before swallowing the first powder, the bania told his wife to stay where she was, so that when he returned after killing the tiger, she could at once give him the second powder and enable him to resume his old shape.

'Well, the bania's plan worked, but only up to a point. He swallowed the first powder and immediately became a magnificent tiger. With a great roar, he bounded towards the man-eater, and after a brief, furious fight, killed his opponent. Then, with his jaws still dripping blood, he returned to his wife.

'The poor girl was terrified and spilt the second powder on the ground. The bania was so angry that he pounced on his wife and killed and ate her. And afterwards, this terrible tiger was so enraged at not being able to become a human again that he killed and ate hundreds of people all over the country.'

'The only people he spared,' added Grandfather, with a twinkle in his eyes, 'were those who owed him money. A bania never gives up a loan as lost, and the tiger still hoped that one day he might become a human again and be able to collect his dues.'

Next morning, when Ramu came back from the well which was used to irrigate his father's fields, he found a crowd of curious children surrounding a jeep and three strangers with guns. Each of the strangers had a gun, and they were accompanied by two bearers and a vast amount of provisions.

They had heard that there was a tiger in the area, and they wanted to shoot it.

One of the hunters, who looked even more strange than the others, had come all the way from America to shoot a tiger, and he vowed that he would not leave the country without a tiger's skin in his baggage. One of his companions had said that he could buy a tiger's skin in Delhi, but the hunter said he preferred to get his own trophies.

These men had money to spend, and as most of the villagers needed money badly, they were only too willing to go into the forest to construct a machan for the hunters. The platform, big enough to take the three men, was put up in the branches of a tall toon, or mahogany, tree.

It was the only night the hunters used the machan. At the end of March, though the days are warm, the nights are still cold. The hunters had neglected to bring blankets, and by midnight, their teeth were chattering. Ramu, having tied up a buffalo calf for them at the foot of the tree, made as if to go home but instead circled the area, hanging up bits and pieces of old clothing on small trees and bushes. He thought he owed that much to the tiger. He knew the wily old king of the jungle would keep well away from the bait if he saw the bits of clothing—for where there were men's clothes, there would be men.

The vigil lasted well into the night but the tiger did not come near the toon tree. Perhaps he wasn't hungry; perhaps he got Ramu's message. In any case, the men in the tree soon gave themselves away.

The cold was really too much for them. A flask of rum was produced, and passed round, and it was not long before there was more purpose to finishing the rum than to finishing off a tiger. Silent at first, the men soon began talking in whispers; and to jungle creatures a human whisper is as telling as a trumpet call.

Soon the men were quite merry, talking in loud voices. And when the first morning light crept over the forest, and Ramu and his friends came back to fetch the great hunters, they found them fast asleep in the machan.

The hunters looked surly and embarrassed as they trudged back to the village.

'No game left in these parts,' said the American.

'Wrong time of the year for tiger,' said the second man.

'Don't know what the country's coming to,' said the third.

And complaining about the weather, the poor quality

of cartridges, the quantity of rum they had drunk, and the perversity of tigers, they drove away in disgust.

It was not until the onset of summer that an event occurred which altered the hunting habits of the old tiger and brought him into conflict with the villagers.

∼

There had been no rain for almost two months, and the tall jungle grass had become a sea of billowy dry yellow. Some refugee settlers, living in an area where the forest had been cleared, had been careless while cooking and had started a jungle fire. Slowly it spread into the interior, from where the acrid smell and the fumes smoked the tiger out towards the edge of the jungle. As night came on, the flames grew more vivid, and the smell stronger. The tiger turned and made for the jheel, where he knew he would be safe provided he swam across to the little island in the centre.

Next morning he was on the island, which was untouched by the fire. But his surroundings had changed. The slopes of the hills were black with burnt grass, and most of the tall bamboo had disappeared. The deer and the wild pig, finding that their natural cover had gone, fled further east.

When the fire had died down and the smoke had cleared, the tiger prowled through the forest again but found no game. Once he came across the body of a burnt rabbit, but he could not eat it. He drank at the jheel and settled down in a shady spot to sleep the day away. Perhaps, by evening, some of the animals would return. If not, he, too, would have to look for new hunting grounds—or new game.

The tiger spent five more days looking for suitable game to kill. By that time he was so hungry that he even resorted to rooting among the dead leaves and burnt out stumps of trees, searching for worms and beetles. This was a sad comedown for the king of the jungle. But even now he hesitated to leave the area, for he had a deep suspicion and fear of the forest further east—forests that were fast being swallowed up by human habitation. He could have gone north, into high mountains, but they did not provide him with the long grass he needed. A panther could manage quite well up there, but not a tiger, who loved the natural privacy of the heavy jungle. In the hills, he would have to hide all the time.

At break of day, the tiger came to the jheel. The water was now shallow and muddy, and a green scum had spread over the top. But it was still drinkable and the tiger quenched his thirst.

He lay down across his favourite rock, hoping for a deer but none came. He was about to get up and go away when he heard an animal approach.

The tiger at once leaped off his perch and flattened himself on the ground, his tawny striped skin merging with the dry grass. A heavy animal was moving through the bushes, and the tiger waited patiently.

A buffalo emerged and came to the water.

The buffalo was alone.

He was a big male, and his long curved horns lay right back across his shoulders. He moved leisurely towards the water, completely unaware of the tiger's presence.

The tiger hesitated before making his charge. It was a

long time—many years—since he had killed a buffalo, and he knew the villagers would not like it. But the pangs of hunger overcame his scruples. There was no morning breeze, everything was still, and the smell of the tiger did not reach the buffalo. A monkey chattered on a nearby tree, but his warning went unheeded.

Crawling stealthily on his stomach, the tiger skirted the edge of the jheel and approached the buffalo from the rear. The waterbirds, who were used to the presence of both animals, did not raise an alarm.

Getting closer, the tiger glanced around to see if there were men, or other buffaloes, in the vicinity. Then, satisfied that he was alone, he crept forward. The buffalo was drinking, standing in shallow water at the edge of the jheel, when the tiger charged from the side and bit deep into the animal's thigh.

The buffalo turned to fight, but the tendons of his right hind leg had been snapped, and he could only stragger forward a few paces. But he was a buffalo—the bravest of the domestic cattle. He was not afraid. He snorted, and lowered his horns at the tiger; but the great cat was too fast, and circling the buffalo, bit into the other hind leg.

The buffalo crashed to the ground, both hind legs crippled, and then the tiger dashed in, using both tooth and claw, biting deep into the buffalo's throat until the blood gushed out from the jugular vein.

The buffalo gave one long, last bellow before dying.

The tiger, having rested, now began to gorge himself, but, even though he had been starving for days, he could not finish the huge carcass. At least one good meal still remained when, satisfied and feeling his strength returning, he quenched his thirst at the jheel. Then he dragged the remains of the buffalo into the bushes to hide it from the vultures, and went off to find a place to sleep.

He would return to the kill when he was hungry.

The villagers were upset when they discovered that a buffalo was missing; and the next day, when Ramu and Shyam came running home to say that they had found the carcass near the jheel, half eaten by a tiger, the men were disturbed and angry. They felt that the tiger had tricked and deceived them. And they knew that once he got a taste for domestic cattle, he would make a habit of slaughtering them.

Kundan Singh, Shyam's father and the owner of the dead buffalo, said he would go after the tiger himself.

'It is all very well to talk about what you will do to the tiger,' said his wife, 'but you should never have let the buffalo go off on its own.'

'He had been out on his own before,' said Kundan. 'This is the first time the tiger has attacked one of our beasts. A devil must have entered the maharaja.'

'He must have been very hungry,' said Shyam.

'Well, we are hungry too,' said Kundan Singh.

'Our best buffalo—the only male in our herd.'

'The tiger will kill again,' said Ramu's father.

'If we let him,' said Kundan.

'Should we send for the shikaris?'

'No. They were not clever. The tiger will escape them easily. Besides, there is no time. The tiger will return for another meal tonight. We must finish him off ourselves!'

'But how?'

Kundan Singh smiled secretively, played with the ends of his moustache for a few moments, and then, with great pride, produced from under his cot a double-barrelled gun of ancient vintage.

'My father bought it from an Englishman,' he said.

'How long ago was that?'

'At the time I was born.'

'And have you ever used it?' asked Ramu's father, who was not sure that the gun would work.

'Well, some years back I let it off at some bandits. You remember the time when those dacoits raided our village? They chose the wrong village, and were severely beaten for their pains. As they left, I fired my gun off at them. They didn't stop running until they crossed the Ganga!'

'Yes, but did you hit anyone?'

'I would have, if someone's goat hadn't got in the way at the last moment. But we had roast mutton that night! Don't worry, brother, I know how the thing fires.'

Accompanied by Ramu's father and some others, Kundan Singh set out for the jheel, where, without shifting the buffalo's carcass—for they knew that the tiger would not come near them if he suspected a trap—they made another machan in the branches of a tall tree some thirty feet from the kill.

Later that evening, Kundan Singh and Ramu's father settled down for the night on their crude platform in the tree.

Several hours passed, and nothing but a jackal was seen by the watchers. And then, just as the moon came up over the distant hills, Kundan and his companion were startled by a low 'A-oonh', followed by a suppressed, rumbling growl.

Kundan grasped his old gun, whilst his friend drew closer to him for comfort. There was complete silence for a minute or two—time that was an agony of suspense for the watchers—and then the sound of stealthy footfalls on dead leaves under the trees.

A moment later, the tiger walked out into the moonlight and stood over his kill.

At first Kundan could do nothing. He was completely overawed by the size of this magnificent tiger. Ramu's father had to nudge him, and then Kundan quickly put the gun to his shoulder, aimed at the tiger's head, and pressed the trigger.

The gun went off with a flash and two loud bangs, as Kundan fired both barrels. Then there was a tremendous roar. One of the bullets had grazed the tiger's head.

The enraged animal rushed at the tree and tried to leap up into the branches. Fortunately the machan had been built at a safe height, and the tiger was unable to reach it. It roared again and then bounded off into the forest.

'What a tiger!' exclaimed Kundan, half in fear and half in admiration. 'I feel as though my liver has turned to water.'

'You missed him completely,' said Ramu's father. 'Your gun makes a big noise; an arrow would have done more damage.'

'I did not miss him,' said Kundan, feeling offended. 'You heard him roar, didn't you? Would he have been so angry if he had not been hit? If I have wounded him badly, he will die.'

'And if you have wounded him slightly, he may turn into a man-eater, and then where will we be?'

'I don't think he will come back,' said Kundan. 'He will

leave these forests.'

They waited until the sun was up before coming down from the tree. They found a few drops of blood on the dry grass but no trail led into the forest, and Ramu's father was convinced that the wound was only a slight one.

The bullet, missing the fatal spot behind the ear, had only grazed the back of the skull and cut a deep groove at its base. It took a few days to heal, and during this time the tiger lay low and did not go near the jheel except when it was very dark and he was very thirsty.

The villagers thought the tiger had gone away, and Ramu and Shyam—accompanied by some other youths, and always carrying axes and lathis—began bringing buffaloes to the jheel again during the day; but they were careful not to let any of them stray far from the herd, and they returned home while it was still daylight.

It was some days since the jungle had been ravaged by the fire, and in the tropics the damage is repaired quickly. In spite of it being the dry season, new life was creeping into the forest.

While the buffaloes wallowed in the muddy water, and the boys wrestled on the grassy island, a big tawny eagle soared high above them, looking for a meal—a sure sign that some of the animals were beginning to return to the forest. It was not long before his keen eyes detected a movement in the glade below.

What the eagle with his powerful eyesight saw was a baby hare, a small fluffy thing, its long pink-tinted ears laid flat along its sides. Had it not been creeping along between two large stones, it would have escaped notice. The eagle waited to see if the mother was about, and as he waited he realized that he was not the only one who coveted this juicy morsel. From the bushes there had appeared a sinuous yellow creature, pressed, low to the ground and moving rapidly towards the hare. It was a yellow jungle cat, hardly noticeable in the scorched grass. With great stealth the jungle cat began to stalk the baby hare.

He pounced. The hare's squeal was cut short by the cat's cruel claws; but it had been heard by the mother hare, who now bounded into the glade and without the slightest hesitation went for the surprised cat.

There was nothing haphazard about the mother hare's attack. She flashed around behind the cat and jumped clean over him. As she landed, she kicked back, sending a stinging jet of dust shooting into the cat's face. She did this again and again.

The bewildered cat, crouching and snarling, picked up the kill and tried to run away with it. But the hare would not permit this. She continued her leaping and buffeting, till eventually the cat, out of sheer frustration, dropped the kill and attacked the mother.

The cat sprang at the hare a score of times, lashing out with his claws; but the mother hare was both clever and agile enough to keep just out of reach of those terrible claws, and drew the cat further and further away from her baby—for she did not as yet know that it was dead.

The tawny eagle saw his chance. Swift and true, he swooped. For a brief moment, as his wings overspread the furry little hare and his talons sank deep into it, he caught a glimpse of the cat racing towards him and the mother hare fleeing into the bushes. And then with a shrill 'kee-ee-ee' of triumph, he rose and whirled away with his dinner.

The boys had heard his shrill cry and looked up just in time to see the eagle flying over the jheel with the small little hare held firmly in his talons.

'Poor hare,' said Shyam. 'Its life was short.'

'That's the law of the jungle,' said Ramu. 'The eagle has a family, too, and must feed it.'

'I wonder if we are any better than animals,' said Shyam.

'Perhaps we are a little better, in some ways,' said Ramu. 'Grandfather always says, "To be able to laugh and to be merciful are the only things that make man better than the beast."'

The next day, while the boys were taking the herd home, one of the buffaloes lagged behind. Ramu did not realize that the animal was missing until he heard an agonized bellow behind him. He glanced over his shoulder just in time to see the big striped tiger dragging the buffalo into a clump of young bamboo. At the same time, the herd became aware of the danger, and the buffaloes snorted with fear as they hurried along the forest path. To urge them forward, and to warn his friends, Ramu cupped his hands to his mouth and gave vent to a yodelling call.

The buffaloes bellowed, the boys shouted, and the birds flew shrieking from the trees. It was almost a stampede by the time the herd emerged from the forest. The villagers heard the thunder of hoofs, and saw the herd coming home amidst clouds of dust and confusion, and knew that something was wrong.

'The tiger!' shouted Ramu. 'He is here! He has killed one of the buffaloes.'

'He is afraid of us no longer,' said Shyam.

'Did you see where he went?' asked Kundan Singh, hurrying up to them.

'I remember the place,' said Ramu. 'He dragged the buffalo in amongst the bamboo.'

'Then there is no time to lose,' said his father. 'Kundan, you take your gun and two men, and wait near the suspension bridge, where the Garur stream joins the Ganga. The jungle is narrow there. We will beat the jungle from our side, and drive the tiger towards you. He will not escape us, unless he swims the river!'

'Good!' said Kundan Singh, running into his house for his gun, with Shyam close at his heels. 'Was it one of our buffaloes again?' he asked.

'It was Ramu's buffalo this time,' said Shyam. 'A good milk buffalo.'

'Then Ramu's father will beat the jungle thoroughly. You boys had better come with me. It will not be safe for you to accompany the beaters.'

Kundan Singh, carrying his gun and accompanied by Ramu, Shyam and two men, headed for the river junction, while Ramu's father collected about twenty men from the village and, guided by one of the boys who had been with Ramu, made for the spot where the tiger had killed the buffalo.

The tiger was still eating when he heard the men coming.

He had not expected to be disturbed so soon. With an angry 'Whoof!' he bounded into a bamboo thicket and watched the men through a screen of leaves and tall grass.

The men did not seem to take much notice of the dead buffalo, but gathered round their leader and held a consultation. Most of them carried hand drums slung from their shoulders. They also carried sticks, spears and axes.

After a hurried conversation, they entered the denser part of the jungle, beating their drums with the palms of their hands. Some of the men banged empty kerosene tins. These made even more noise than the drums.

The tiger did not like the noise and retreated deeper into the jungle. But he was surprised to find that the men, instead of going away, came after him into the jungle, banging away on their drums and tins, and shouting at the top of their voices. They had separated now, and advanced single or in pairs, but nowhere were they more than fifteen yards apart. The tiger could easily have broken through this slowly advancing semicircle of men—one swift blow from his paw would have felled the strongest of them—but his main aim was to get away from the noise. He hated and feared noise made by men.

He was not a man-eater and he would not attack a man unless he was very angry or frightened or very desperate; and he was none of these things as yet. He had eaten well, and he would have liked to rest in peace—but there would be no rest for any animal until the men ceased their tremendous clatter and din.

For an hour Ramu's father and the others beat the jungle,

calling, drumming and trampling the undergrowth. The tiger had no rest. Whenever he was able to put some distance between himself and the men, he would sink down in some shady spot to rest; but, within five or ten minutes, the trampling and drumming would sound nearer, and the tiger, with an angry snarl, would get up and pad north, pad silently north along the narrowing strip of jungle, towards the junction of the Garur stream and the Ganga. Ten years ago, he would have had the jungle on his right in which to hide; but the trees had been felled long ago to make way for humans and houses, and now he could only move to the left, towards the river.

It was about noon when the tiger finally appeared in the open. He longed for the darkness and security of the night, for the sun was his enemy. Kundan and the boys had a clear view of him as he stalked slowly along—now in the open with the sun glinting on his glossy hide, now in the shade or passing through the shorter reeds. He was still out of range of Kundan's gun, but there was no fear of his getting out of the beat, as the 'stops' were all picked men from the village. He disappeared among some bushes but soon reappeared to retrace his steps, the beaters having done their work well. He was now only one hundred and fifty yards from the rocks where Kundan Singh waited, and he looked very big.

The beat had closed in, and the exit along the bank downstream was completely blocked, so the tiger turned and disappeared into a belt of reeds, and Kundan Singh expected that the head would soon peer out of the cover a few yards away. The beaters were now making a great noise, shouting and beating their drums, but nothing moved; and Ramu, watching from a distance, wondered, 'Has he slipped through the beaters?' And he half hoped so.

Tins clashed, drums beat, and some of the men poked into the reeds with their spears or long bamboos. Perhaps one of these thrusts found a mark, because at last the tiger was roused, and with an angry desperate snarl, he charged out of the reeds, splashing his way through an inlet of mud and water. Kundan Singh fired, and his bullet struck the tiger on the thigh.

The mighty animal stumbled; but he was up in a minute, and rushing through a gap in the narrowing line of beaters, he made straight for the only way across the river—the suspension bridge that passed over the Ganga here, providing a route into the high hills beyond.

'We'll get him now,' said Kundan, priming his gun again. 'He's right in the open!'

The suspension bridge swayed and trembled as the wounded tiger lurched across it. Kundan fired, and this time the bullet grazed the tiger's shoulder. The animal bounded forward, lost his footing on the unfamiliar, slippery planks of the swaying bridge, and went over the side, falling headlong into the strong, swirling waters of the river.

He rose to the surface once, but the current took him under and away, and only a thin streak of blood remained on the river's surface.

Kundan and others hurried downstream to see if the dead tiger had been washed up on the river's banks; but though they searched the riverside for several miles, they did not find the king of the forest.

He had not provided anyone with a trophy. His skin would not be spread on a couch, nor would his head be hung up on a wall. No claw of his would be hung as a charm round the neck of a child. No villager would use his fat as a cure for rheumatism.

~

At first the villagers were glad because they felt their buffaloes were safe. Then the men began to feel that something had gone out of their lives, out of the life of the forest; they began to feel that the forest was no longer a forest. It had been shrinking year by year, but, as long as the tiger had been there and the villagers had heard it roar at night, they had known that they were still secure from the intruders and newcomers who came to fell the trees and eat up the land and let the flood waters into the village. But now that the tiger had gone, it was as though a protector had gone, leaving the forest open and vulnerable, easily destroyable. And once the forest was destroyed they, too, would be in danger...

There was another thing that had gone with the tiger, another thing that had been lost, a thing that was being lost everywhere—something called 'nobility'.

Ramu remembered something that his grandfather had once said. 'The tiger is the very soul of India, and when the last tiger goes, so will the soul of the country.'

The boys lay flat on their stomachs on their little mud island and watched the monsoon clouds gathering overhead.

'The king of our forest is dead,' said Shyam. 'There are no more tigers.'

'There must be tigers,' said Ramu. 'How can there be an India without tigers?'

The river had carried the tiger many miles away from his home, from the forest he had always known, and brought him ashore on a strip of warm yellow sand, where he lay in the sun, quite still, but breathing.

Vultures gathered and waited at a distance, some of them perching on the branches of nearby trees.

But the tiger was more drowned than hurt, and as the river water oozed out of his mouth, and the warm sun made new life throb through his body, he stirred and stretched, and his glazed eyes came into focus. Raising his head, he saw trees and tall grass.

Slowly he heaved himself off the ground and moved at a crouch to where the grass waved in the afternoon breeze. Would he be harried again, and shot at? There was no smell of man. The tiger moved forward with greater confidence.

There was, however, another smell in the air—a smell that reached back to the time when he was young and fresh and full of vigour—a smell that he had almost forgotten but could never quite forget: the smell of a tigress!

He raised his head high, and new life surged through his tired limbs. He gave a full-throated roar and moved purposefully through the tall grass. And the roar came back to him, calling him, calling him forward: a roar that meant there would be more tigers in the land!

RAINDROP

~

This leaf, so complete in itself,
Is only part of the tree.
And this tree, so complete in itself,
Is only part of the forest.
And the forest runs down the hill to the sea,
And the sea, so complete in itself,
Rests like a raindrop
In the hands of God.